"It's been twenty years," **Merrick said. "The irony is you don't look a helluva lot different."**

Johanna looked away, then turned back and raised her chin. "Perhaps it's the fugitive lifestyle that agrees with me. Or being pampered by lies, and deceived by rogue agents out for revenge on my husb—" She cut herself off.

"Husband?"

"Not for long."

She had a right to be angry, but dammit, so did he. He tried not to notice how short her towel was. Tried unsuccessfully. He knew every inch of her body. He'd dreamed of her so often he could envision every curve beneath that damn towel.

In that moment all he wanted to do was pick her up and claim his wife.

Dear Reader,

I'd like to say I've saved the best for last in this seventh and final book in my SPY GAMES miniseries. And yet each book in this series has been special to me in so many ways. As I began to delve into Adolf Merrick's character with all his trials and all his grief, I realized what a treasure he was. Once a government assassin, now the commander of the NSA Onyxx Agency, he's a man who has truly survived hell.

They say survival is everything. That justice will come to those both good and evil. That the journey makes you or breaks you. I admit that the inception of this story was based on survival and justice, but as I joined Merrick in his eleventh hour, it became evident that his journey was a resurrection of heart and soul. For a man's valor and redemption are weighed by his undying loyalty, honor, trust and his humanity to forgive.

Come with me on this final leg of SPY GAMES. My hope is that you fall in love with Merrick as I did. His broken heart has been waiting a long time to be set free.
For even the deepest wounds can be healed by a miracle.
So yes, perhaps I have saved the best for last. If you missed one of the previous SPY GAMES books, log on to www.wendyrosnau.com.

Until next time,

Wendy Rosnau

WENDY ROSNAU

Merrick's Eleventh Hour

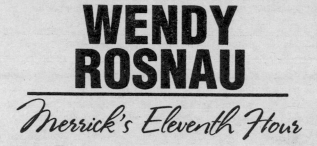

Silhouette®
Romantic
SUSPENSE

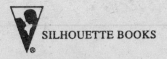 SILHOUETTE BOOKS

Recycling programs
for this product may
not exist in your area.

ISBN-13: 978-0-373-27611-0
ISBN-10:   0-373-27611-7

MERRICK'S ELEVENTH HOUR

Books by Wendy Rosnau

Silhouette Romantic Suspense

The Long Hot Summer #996
A Younger Woman #1074
The Right Side of the Law #1110
*Beneath the Silk #1157
*One Way Out #1211
*Last Man Standing #1227
†Perfect Assassin #1384
†Undercover Nightingale #1436
†Sleeping with Danger #1489
†Merrick's Eleventh Hour #1541

Silhouette Bombshell

The Spy Wore Red #32
The Spy with the Silver Lining #89

Silhouette Books

†A Thousand Kisses Deep

Stuck on You
  "Just Say Yes"

*The Brotherhood
†Spy Games

WENDY ROSNAU

resides on sixty secluded acres in Minnesota with her husband and their two children. She divides her time between her family-owned bookstore and writing romantic suspense. Her first book, *The Long Hot Summer,* was a *Romantic Times BOOKreviews* nominee for Best First Series Romance of 2000. Her third book, *The Right Side of the Law,* was a *Romantic Times BOOKreviews* Top Pick. She received the Midwest Fiction Writers 2001 Rising Star Award. Wendy loves to hear from her readers. Visit her Web site at www.wendyrosnau.com.

For Tyler and Jen. No mother could
be more blessed. You are my
greatest fortune and priority.

A special thank-you to Joyce Alt
for her expertise on asthma.
Any inaccuracies are mine alone.

Chapter 1

An amputee for twenty-two years, Peter Briggs had a certain routine—work at eight, supper at seven, in bed by nine. But the flu had disrupted his staid life for the past week. At 10:30 p.m. he rolled his wheelchair out of the bathroom and into the bedroom for the third time that night.

Weak and nauseated, he reached for the bar that hung above his bed and hoisted himself onto the mattress. Snuggled beneath the blankets, conscious of his old routine, he slid his hand beneath the pillow, his fingers brushing the cool steel of a 9mm SIG. A grunt of assurance, a moan, then exhaustion sent Peter into a restless sleep.

An hour later he woke up shivering, his body racked with chills. He pulled the blanket up around his neck, and that was when he noticed how cold the air was. If he hadn't known better he'd have thought the heat had been shut off in his D.C. apartment.

Peter reached for the bar overhead and pulled himself up.

He turned on the lamp, and found the source of his discomfort. The window was open, a stiff breeze whipping the lacy beige curtain into a ghostly dance, driving in the cold April rain all over the floor.

He was staring at the open window in a confused daze when he heard a noise in the living room. Instinct sent his hand under his pillow to retrieve the SIG, at the same time he reached out to his wheelchair.

No SIG.

No wheelchair.

As if his rising panic summoned his lifeline, the bedroom door opened and his wheelchair rolled slowly inside.

The smell of vomit and diarrhea was caustic. It had turned the small apartment into a war zone. Cyrus Krizova leaned back in the wheelchair and studied his old comrade on the narrow bed. The SIG in his lap, he said, "You look like hell, Briggs. Rough week?"

"The worst of my life."

Cyrus's dark eyes shifted to the lower half of the bed where Peter's legs should have been. "I doubt that. I imagine you've had plenty of dark days."

Peter rubbed his eyes, rheumy from lack of sleep. "You haven't left Greece in years. What brings you to Washington?"

"Merrick has uncovered our little secret."

"That's impossible. There's no data to prove it. I've been careful."

"That's good to hear. But he's looking for that nonexistent data. I suppose I'm going to have to take credit for that. Still, I believe I only confirmed what he suspected. Onyxx has been looking for a mole inside the Agency for some time."

"You told him it's me?"

"He's been leaving you out of the loop for months. That's why you weren't able to warn me when he arrived in Greece and stole my prisoners from Vouno weeks ago. Not to mention his untimely arrival at Lesvago days later."

"I had nothing to do with that."

"My point. You've been isolated. Merrick's unscheduled raid cost me billions, as well as my daughter. Melita has defected to the enemy's camp."

Beads of perspiration popped out on Peter's forehead. "I had no idea Merrick had left Washington until he'd returned. If you need someone to blame, blame that bastard Sully Paxton. You should have killed him a long time ago."

"What I should have done is irrelevant now. You really don't understand this little parody you've been living this past week, do you?"

"I contracted the flu. I—"

"The flu is it?" Cyrus smiled. "The infection running through your body is no flu strain. It's a manufactured virus. Think, Briggs. Where were you the night you took ill?"

"I was at Chadwick's. Merrick took me to dinner."

"Go to dinner with him often?"

"No."

"You're a fool, Briggs." Cyrus sighed. "And Chadwick's of all places. Where Ames sold out the CIA and gave up the names of twenty agents to the Russians. Where moles and traitors hand off government secrets and stab their comrades in the back."

The look on Peter's face was priceless. "Merrick poisoned me at Chadwick's?"

"Must I remind you that, before Onyxx, Merrick was a class-A government assassin? His bag of tricks far exceeds a simple bullet between the eyes. As much as it pains me to admit, Icis is still the best in the business. I would have died at Lesvago if I hadn't been wearing a bulletproof vest."

"I'm going to die?"

"If he wanted you dead, you would be. No, Merrick believes you'll join him in the hunt for me to save your own skin once he's found proof you've been filching information."

"He won't find anything, and I'd never give you up. Haven't I proven my loyalty?"

"Loyalty that served your own revenge. You begged Merrick for your life in Prague and he gave it to you. Had he chosen to save me instead, I would never have betrayed him."

"Why do you care why I agreed to be your mole? My reasons still served your purpose."

"Treason is a tricky business." Cyrus stood and checked the SIG's ammunition clip. The weapon showed a full eight rounds.

"What are you doing?"

"I considered making this look like a suicide. A man chained to a wheelchair must have contemplated it over the years, but you know how much I enjoy tormenting Merrick."

"I can still be of use to you."

"Come now, Briggs, you had to know your days were numbered."

"Not like this, Cyrus. At least let me get dressed and give me my chair. Let me die with some dignity."

"A traitor has no dignity. Good-bye, Briggs."

Cyrus raised the SIG and fired. The first two bullets plowed through Peter's skull, out the back of his head and into the wall. The third went into his heart and stayed there.

Traitor, mole, comrade… None of it mattered now. Peter Briggs was dead before his head hit the pillow.

Hours later, Cyrus Krizova, aka the Chameleon, boarded a plane back to Greece. Like a soldier heading home from the war, a little victory celebration was definitely in order.

Da, the spoils of war.

For two decades Adolf Merrick had coveted the dream.

Johanna's image came first. Long raven-black hair surrounding a delicate oval face. Perfectly arched eyebrows framing hazel-green eyes. The body of a temptress that moved with the regal grace of a cat.

Merrick flattened out his hand and stroked the white satin

sheet, remembering the way she liked to curl up next to him. The exotic scent of Medallion roses had steeped the air, their peach petals exploiting the memories. The crackle and pop of wood burning slow and luminous in the brick fireplace fueling another timeless image.

Eyes closed, drunk on recall, he beckoned for her to come to him. And like a whisper riding a gentle breeze, Johanna came for a visit.

The bed moved against her fragile weight. Her moist breath teasing his neck, she whispered, *However you want me, I'm here.*

Merrick moaned deep into the vortex of the dream—a dream he would live in 24/7 if that were possible. He arched his hips in silent solicitation. Rewarded with a naked thigh sliding over his hips.

Then she leaned forward and kissed him.

The kiss of life.

The kiss of death.

Stay focused.

Don't wake up.

However you want me, I'm here.

He wanted her hot and mind-blowing. He wanted her all night. Every night. He wanted time to stand still. No, he wanted to rewind time and go back to the beginning.

Take me back, my love. My wife. My life.

Stay focused.

Don't wake up.

Another kiss.

Another moan.

Another night wrapped in ghostly arms.

No more thinking. No more sorrow. No more tears.

Nothing but the dream. Nothing but the memories. Nothing but Johanna swallowing him up body and soul and taking him on a wicked midnight ride.

* * *

The incessant rain tapping at the window like an unwelcome voyeur roused Merrick. It was dawn, another dreary, rainy day in April. He tossed back the white satin sheet, soiled now from making love to his ghostly wife. He dropped his feet to the floor and rubbed the gray stubble along his rugged jaw.

The fire had died sometime in the middle of the night, but not the memories. He realized now that he should have hired someone to box up Johanna's things. Her clothes still hung in the closet. Her jewelry box on the vanity. The quilt she'd made for their bed was still folded over the rocker—all of it wrapped in cobwebs, surrounded by yellowed curtains, peeling wallpaper and wood floors stained from a leaky roof.

The tattered remains of heaven on earth.

He should have sold the house years ago, before it became an eyesore. He'd planned to, but he had always come up with some lame-ass excuse.

He shoved himself up from the bed and walked naked into the bathroom with a powerful grace that, at age fifty-two, still garnered him a second look from a beautiful woman. By society's standards Adolf Merrick was one of the lucky ones. Like a renowned bottle of port years in the making, he seemed to get better with age.

The only evidence that he was past his prime was his silver hair—a phenomenon that had happened virtually overnight following Johanna's death.

He turned on the shower and stepped inside. He kept the water cold—a strategic maneuver to quash the residual effects of making love to Johanna's ghost. Five minutes later, back on track, with a towel wrapped low around his hips, he headed for the kitchen.

The windows faced Johanna's rose garden in the backyard, and when she hadn't been sharing his bed at night, or cooking something fabulous for dinner, he would find her in the garden with her roses. He'd left the windows open last night, and he could smell the heavy sweet fragrance—the scent as caustic as the memories.

His cell phone rang while he was cooking the hell out of a cup of instant coffee in the microwave—after all this time he still couldn't brew a decent pot of coffee. He backtracked to the bedroom and picked up his phone from the nightstand, checked the number and saw it was Sly McEwen.

"What's up?"

"I've got bad news."

Merrick heard the distress in Sly's voice. "Let's hear it."

"Peter Briggs is dead and so is the operative we had staked out in front of his apartment. That's all I know. No details. The Agency called me after they couldn't reach you."

"I must have been in the shower."

"I'm on my way to Briggs's apartment now. My guess is Krizova sent Holic Reznik to clean up a loose end. Maybe we should have locked Briggs up."

Merrick hadn't wanted to do that. As of yet they hadn't been able to prove that Briggs was guilty of treason. They needed concrete evidence, and that had been damn hard to come by.

"When should I expect you?" Sly asked.

"One hour. I'm at my country house."

"I thought you sold that old monster years ago."

Merrick set his jaw, sidestepped the issue, as well as his personal obsession with the *old monster,* saying, "Damn good thing I didn't or I'd be homeless, thanks to Krizova blowing up my apartment. I don't want Briggs's body touched until I get there. One hour."

The country house was north of D.C. As Merrick drove through the rain, he called Jacy Madox and got him out of bed in Montana. Since he'd slipped the flu virus into Briggs's wine a week ago, Jacy had been going through the data on Peter's computer while he was housebound. Although Jacy's field agent days were over, he continued to work for Onyxx from his mountain home miles from nowhere. A cybergenius, he was considered one of the best hackers in the intelligence world.

"Sorry about Briggs," Jacy said. "The news is I didn't find anything on his computer. If he was Krizova's mole, he left no evidence behind."

"All right. I'll be in touch."

Merrick hung up, his mood sinking past sour. It was starting to look like finding Cyrus's latest hideout was going to take an act of God. Not that he wasn't thankful for the surprise resurrection of Sully Paxton two months ago. After believing his agent was dead, Merrick had learned that Sully had given new meaning to the word *survival.* It had been the salt the Agency needed to step up their commitment to ending Cyrus's fanaticism with Onyxx, as well as his global terrorism.

With Sully's help they'd found two of Krizova's compounds in Greece, rescued more than a dozen government agents imprisoned in the bowels of one of his monastery hideouts and recovered a cache of weapons bound for rebel hands. They had also rescued Melita Krizova from Cyrus's warped sense of fatherly love.

But at the end of the day—once again—Cyrus had managed to elude capture.

Sully Paxton was still in Greece, on the island of Amorgós with Melita. He'd been tirelessly combing the islands trying to pinpoint Cyrus's latest hideout. He would need to fill Sully in on the recent turn of events, but he'd wait until he had all the facts.

Merrick swung his black Jag to the curb of the ten-story apartment building where Peter Briggs had lived for the past twenty-two years, since the Prague incident. Out front Pierce Fourtier and Ash Kelly, two of his elite Rat Fighters, were standing under the awning smoking.

Pulling up the collar on his black leather jacket to combat the rain, he joined them. "Got a name on our stakeout agent?"

"New guy. Nathan Connor. Shot three times, just like Briggs," Ash said.

"Sly's inside," Pierce offered.

Merrick nodded and headed in. Peter's apartment was on the ground floor, halfway down the hall. He walked through the open door. Sly McEwen was standing at the window, his stance in sync with his serious attitude. Over six feet, rock-solid, Sly had proven himself to be a man you could count on. He didn't know what the word *quit* meant, and Merrick liked that about him. It's why he'd made him his second in command.

Sly turned from the window and motioned to the bedroom. "Nothing's been touched. I called Harry Pendleton and gave him the news. Nathan Connor was his nephew. The kid was twenty-three. Onyxx activated him six months ago."

"I thought I recognized the name." Merrick walked through the living room and headed for the bedroom. Briggs's body should have been his primary focus, but instead his eyes locked on the peach-colored roses in a crystal vase on the nightstand.

There was only one flower shop in D.C. where you could buy Medallion roses without placing a special order. Merrick knew that because they had been Johanna's favorite and he regularly purchased the rare hybrid to place on her grave.

Merrick left Sly with the task of seeing to Peter's body and, twenty minutes after his arrival, he was on his way to Finny Floral. Sarah Finny lived in the apartment above the flower shop, and when he pulled up he noticed that the Open sign was on in the window. He leapt from the car and crossed the street. As he passed the window he saw her standing behind the counter waiting on a plump bald man in a gray suit. The little bell rang above the door as he swung it open.

She glanced up, saw him, then turned back to the elderly

gentleman. There was no surprise in her soft brown eyes when she'd seen him, which told Merrick she'd been expecting him.

The bald gentleman left with his purchase, and Merrick stepped up to the counter. Before he could say anything, Sarah spoke.

"You've come about the Medallions. The ones *he* bought yesterday."

"What did he look like, Sarah?"

"Very tall, with dark gray hair. Not silver like yours. And shorter." She glanced at the overnight shadow on Merrick's jaw. "Clean shaven. He had a nasty scar," she touched her neck, "here."

Merrick had been expecting her to describe the scrawny build of Holic Reznik, a hired assassin who had become involved in Cyrus's nefarious activities years ago. Instead she'd given him a description of Krizova himself.

"I wanted to call you yesterday, but he said if I did he would be back for more than roses. I was afraid, Adolf. Did I make a mistake?"

"No, you did the right thing. Tell me exactly what he said."

"He asked for three dozen Medallions, one dozen in a crystal vase."

"Three dozen?"

"Yes."

"What time was he here?"

"Yesterday around two o'clock. I remember because I was getting a large order together for a wedding that had to be delivered by four." She opened a drawer and pulled out a small, three-inch-square brown envelope. "He told me when you came by to give you this."

Merrick took the envelope and peeled open the seal. He pinched the envelope and looked inside. He was careful not to react to the contents, resealed the envelope and slid it into his jacket pocket.

"So he bought the roses, gave you the envelope and told you I'd be by today? That's it?"

She pointed to a small gift-card display on the counter. "He bought a card."

Merrick glanced at the card rack. There had been no card with the vase of flowers at Peter's apartment.

"Adolf, what's going on?"

If Cyrus intended to kill Sarah, he would. Merrick wasn't going to cause her more distress by telling her that, but within the hour she'd have an invisible bodyguard. "You're not in any danger," he said. "I've got to go." He started to leave.

"Adolf?"

He turned back.

"If you need me to deliver Johanna's roses to the cemetery the next time you're out of town, you know you can ask. Just because we're not seeing each other anymore doesn't mean we can't remain friends."

Over the past three years their friendship had slowly resolved into casual dinners. Sarah wanted more, and he'd been on the verge of giving it to her until Cyrus had blown up his apartment. Once that had happened, he realized that putting Sarah in his life meant he would be putting her in Krizova's iron sights, as well.

He hadn't explained it that way to her. Government spies and espionage weren't exactly dinner table conversation. Fifteen years her senior, he'd taken a different approach the day he'd stopped seeing her.

She stepped around the counter. She was wearing a pale-blue blouse and black skirt, her blond hair twisted up off her neck. She was the exact opposite of Johanna. It was the first thing he always thought about when he looked at Sarah—his lovely ghost wasn't just content to haunt him at night—and perhaps that was the real reason he'd ended it.

"No strings, Adolf. You know how I feel about you, but I respect your decision."

"You're a good friend, Sarah. I'll be leaving town soon. Maybe you could see to the roses for the next couple of Saturdays."

She nodded. "I'll see to it that Johanna gets them."

He leaned forward and kissed her cheek. "Thank you."

He left the flower shop with the envelope burning a hole in his pocket. It was still raining, the day surrendering to a bleak sky of gray clouds and a bitter chill in the air. Inside the car, Merrick slipped his hand into his pocket and pulled out the envelope. He dropped the ring into his hand— Johanna's wedding ring—and closed his eyes. He remembered the day he'd bought it, and with that memory came the memory of her death. The anniversary of that fateful day was looming. It had been twenty years and it still felt like yesterday.

Because he knew Cyrus didn't do anything without a reason, he had to ask himself, why had he kept the ring, and why was he giving it back to him now?

Merrick swore, returned the ring to the envelope, then to his pocket. He started the car, glanced across the street. Sarah was standing in the window.

He drove the Jag out into the traffic and the rain. Cyrus had bought three dozen roses. He'd left one dozen at Peter's apartment. There was no doubt in his mind where he would find the other two.

Forty minutes later, Merrick parked at the Oak Hill Cemetery and walked through the rain down the path to Johanna's grave. Before he reached it, he saw the roses in the cone-shaped brass vase.

The stark white card was pierced on a rose thorn like a dagger. He bent down and pulled the card free. The rain had smeared the ink, but it was still legible.

Four words scribbled in red ink. Four words that would send Merrick back to Greece.

Game on. Your move.

Chapter 2

"Kipler has just sent word that the *Starina* has been spotted, Callia. Your husband is home."

Cyrus's long-standing housekeeper, Zeta Poulos, stood in the bedroom doorway, her pretty island features accented by her smile.

The sun was setting. Callia had just showered and slipped on a white caftan. With no time to dress, she tucked her asthma inhaler in the nightstand drawer along with her nebulizer, then stepped out onto the veranda.

The view from the second-story bedroom was picture-perfect. A vision of paradise that would easily sell a dream vacation to Corfu.

Three months ago Cyrus had moved her and Erik into a villa on the island. She was used to being uprooted. Survival came with a price, and that price had required a new address every couple of years.

The cove was normally quiet, but now six guards scrambled toward the dock as the *Starina* glided into the harbor. Cyrus came ashore quickly. He spoke to Timon Kipler, the man in charge when her husband was away, and the exchange sent Kipler hurrying back to the yacht.

The warm island breeze blew Callia's black hair into her eyes and she reached up. Holding her hair in place, she watched Cyrus begin the long climb up the stone steps that wrapped the sharp, rocky face where the villa was perched like an eagle's nest high above the Ionian Sea.

Her movement must have caught his attention, and he stopped and looked up. He was still a hundred yards away, but she knew he was smiling. He gave her a thumbs-up—the signal that all was well, and she waved in relief.

He never spoke about business. It was an old rule that had come into play long ago. A rule she never challenged. As long as he came back, she was content. And he always came back. It was the one constant in her life. That, and Erik.

In the beginning she'd felt only gratitude, indebted to him for saving her life. But over the years her gratitude had slowly turned into love. Not the kind born out of burning passion. This was a safe and secure love bred out of loyalty and trust.

When he disappeared from sight, she remained on the veranda. She heard him speaking to Zeta. The fifty-year-old housekeeper spoke softly in return. Cyrus never let the smallest detail of their lives go unchecked. Whether it had to do with his business affairs or mundane household trivia, he required an accounting from everyone he employed.

She heard his footsteps on the stone tiles that were polished like a mirror. Caught the scent of sweet tobacco, but she didn't turn around. Then a pair of strong arms captured her around the waist.

He lowered his head, said softly, "Although I have no sympathy for the weaknesses of men, I confess you are mine."

Callia smiled. "Have you taken to reciting poetry after all these years?"

"Poetry? I know nothing about poetry," he muttered close to her ears. "Greek mythology, perhaps. Inspired by your goddesslike beauty."

He hugged her tighter, drew her back against his hard body, and she knew his eyes had drifted shut. Knew that she held some odd power over him, that she was his weakness. And although he had no sympathy for men with such flaws, she had become her husband's debility.

"It's hard to believe that you could have grown more beautiful. Have you and Zeta cooked up some fountain of youth potion you've neglected to tell me about? Something we could bottle and sell to the islanders?"

Still smiling, Callia turned in his arms. "If you're trying to get me in bed, you don't need to use flattery."

"Is that what I'm doing, trying to get you in bed?"

"That's usually where you want me when you first come home. A new routine tonight?"

"No. I like the old routine."

"That's why you're staring at my mouth?"

"You always kiss me right about now. *Da,* I like the old routine. So where is my welcome-home kiss, wife?"

Callia went up on her tiptoes, one hand curling around his neck as she offered him a warm kiss. When she would have pulled away, he slid his hands over her backside and pulled her into him, lengthening the kiss.

She was naked beneath the flimsy caftan. He released a primal moan, then let her go.

"Give me a quick update on Erik so I can concentrate on my wife."

"He's still opposing college," she said, giving way to her disappointment and frustration over her most recent argument with her son. "He wants to work with you."

"And that frightens you?"

"Shouldn't it?"

"You know I would never let anything happen to our son."

"Can you please talk to him."

"You mean change his mind?"

"Please?"

"I'll speak to him. I see you've already started working your magic on decorating the villa. Not overdoing it are you?"

"No. I'm fine."

"Fine isn't wonderful. Zeta told me you had an asthma attack a few days ago."

"Spring pollen," she said to dismiss the incident that had put her on her back for two days. She still wasn't feeling a hundred percent—it would take days—but she would deal with it as she always had, without complaint. "So you like what I'm doing with the house?"

"I like whatever you like. The villa is adequate. Soon to be beautiful. Whatever you want."

"You spoil me."

"I have an ulterior motive. A spoilt wife is happy and content." He cupped her face and kissed her again. "A man would have to be crazy not to give you whatever you wanted, just to be in the company of that smile. Now then, what were you saying about our routine?"

He liked it when she made the first move. Dutifully, she reached up and began unbuttoning his shirt. Three buttons open and she spotted an angry red scar that hadn't yet healed completely. "What happened?"

"A minor accident. A careless mistake."

"You're never careless." She stepped away from him, reluctant to ask him what had happened, but needing some kind of assurance that nothing had changed. That they were still safe. "Who did that to you?"

She saw his eyebrows furrow. "You know the rules, and you know by now that I'm indestructible."

He left her standing on the veranda and walked back into the bedroom. He removed his shirt, and she saw more scars overlapping the old ones that had ravaged his body years ago.

Some horrible injustice—a betrayal before they had met—is how he'd explained what had to have been a near death experience.

Callia understood betrayal. Her own had left her scarred, and although the wounds weren't visible, she'd been cut deeply and forever changed.

She stepped into the bedroom, still watching him. Naked, he tossed the gold coverlet off the bed and stretched out on the blue satin sheets.

"Show me, Callia. Show your husband how beautiful you are. I want to feast my eyes on every inch of you. I've thought of nothing else the entire time I've been away."

She slid the caftan off her slender shoulders and let it fall to the floor. For a woman in her forties, she was still trim, her breasts high and firm, her curvy body and slender legs toned like an athlete from years of long walks on the guarded beaches of Greece.

His eyes moved slowly over her as she came to him and curled up beside him. She knew he liked to be touched, and again she made the first move, gliding her fingers gently over his bare chest. Then lower.

A moan of pleasure made his eyes drift shut. "That's it, work your magic."

"You're tired. You should sleep."

When his eyes remained closed and he didn't answer, she attempted to leave the bed, but his hand snaked out and gripped her wrist. Eyes open, he said, "Straddle me, Callia. I'll sleep later."

With Merrick's duties at Onyxx left in Sly McEwen's capable hands, and Harry Pendleton's blessing, he prepared to leave for Greece. He made a quick trip back to the country house to pack, then arrived at the airport early in the afternoon. Before he boarded the plane he called Sully Paxton to apprise him of the recent turn of events.

"I'm flying to Rome. I don't want to give Cyrus a heads-up, so I intend to avoid the airport in Athens. He's probably got it staked out. We both know why he wants me back in Greece. He's expecting me to lead him to you and Melita."

"You know he's left someone behind in Washington to follow you."

"They won't be on my ass for long. I want to talk to Melita when I get there."

"The report I sent you was complete. She answered every one of your questions about Cyrus to the best of her knowledge. Remember, Melita grew up in a bubble. One that Cyrus built around her. He kept her in the dark on his business affairs, and virtually a prisoner at Lesvago until he moved her to Despotiko. We know more about the bastard than his own daughter does."

"I'd still like to talk to her. Maybe a few new questions might spark a memory that could help us find him. It's all we have right now." Merrick gave Sully some last-minute instructions. "Send your man Hector to Crete with a boat. Tell him to leave it in Iráklion for me."

"It'll be there. Have a safe trip."

The flight left on schedule. Merrick forced himself to sleep on the plane knowing that when he arrived in Greece his days and nights would be rolled into one. He reached Rome after a rough trip over the ocean. Three people on the plane from Washington took the same flight to Iráklion on the island of Crete. Two businessmen and one woman.

Merrick rented a room at a resort hotel, changed clothes and waited for the cover of night. Leaning on a cane, dressed as if he were years older, he shuffled his feet toward a taxi and instructed the driver to take him to the harbor.

As Sully Paxton had promised, Hector had left a sixty-foot sport cruiser christened *Aldora*—winged gift—for him. Hector had been a guard at Despotiko during Melita and Sully's incarceration. More loyal to Melita than Cyrus,

Hector had been an integral part in her escape with Sully months ago. Since then he had remained with them on Amorgós.

Sure no one had followed him, Merrick boarded the *Aldora* and sped away into the night in the gutsy twelve-hundred-horsepower yacht. She had a lean underbelly, an enclosed cockpit, one stateroom, a bathroom and galley—everything a man would need to survive months at sea.

An hour before dawn, Merrick reached Amorgós. He spotted the villa on the southeast coast. When he reached the hidden cove, he saw Sully's wicked speed-demon cruiser moored in the harbor. He studied the villa on the top of a rugged hillside. Sully had chosen the spot with strategy in mind. No one could enter the cove without being seen. Already Sully Paxton was heading down the hillside, that silly little goat of Melita's trailing him in the moonlight.

Merrick leaned into the dock railing as Sully came toward him.

"Were you followed from D.C.?" Sully asked.

"All the way to Crete. No problem after that. They weren't looking for an old man with arthritis."

They shared a grin.

"Did you tell Melita I wanted to talk to her?"

"I did. But like I said, I don't think you're going to learn much that we don't already know. She lived at Lesvago with Simon when she was growing up. They were raised by maids and housekeepers. Cyrus popped in now and then. She says she spent one week once every other year with Cyrus and his wife and her half brother, but the visits were always on a different island."

The look on Sully's face made his dark Irish expression even more foreboding than usual. Melita's life as Cyrus's daughter had been no life at all. A virtual prisoner since he had killed her mother and taken her and Simon to Lesvago on the island of Mykonos. She'd been eight at the time.

Sully said, "I've been combing the islands for weeks, and I don't have one damn lead on Cyrus's current hideout."

Cyrus's corrupt activities had made him a wealthy man and allowed him to set up a maze of compounds throughout Greece. From a strategist's standpoint, the islands were the perfect mecca for a criminal to hide and never be found.

"When can I talk to Melita?"

"She's sleeping. Why don't you catch a few hours yourself? You look beat. I'll bring her to you when she wakes up."

Merrick returned to the *Aldora,* but he never slept. He unpacked his duffel bag, tossed his shaving kit in the bathroom and his clothes in the drawers beneath the double-wide berth. All the comforts of home, he thought. Sully had even stocked the galley.

He never went anywhere without the picture of Johanna in the garden at the country house, and he pulled it from his duffel and laid it on the table as he entered the galley. He'd snapped the picture in the backyard a few months before her death. Johanna was standing among the roses wearing jeans on her narrow hips and a lavender silk blouse. She was smelling the roses, her hand holding back her long hair from her face.

Feeling like a caged animal, he headed up the companionway and left the *Aldora* to stroll the beach. He'd been traveling nonstop and was dog-ass tired, but his adrenalin was pumping. For some unexplained reason he felt he was about to learn something crucial that would put him back on the scent of his enemy.

Maybe it was just wishful thinking, but he'd always felt as though Melita was the key to finding Cyrus. She knew something, even if she wasn't aware of it.

With the scent of his wife lingering on his body, Cyrus rose early. He grabbed his black robe off the chair and pulled it on. Callia was stilled curled up on the bed after he'd had her every way imaginable. The smile he wore as he left the room was that of a prevailing conqueror. The sex had been carnal, fueled by a rapturous hunger that would never be quenched.

Sated temporarily, he focused on his game of cat-and-mouse with Merrick. Soon his old buddy would return to Greece and lead him to Sully and Melita.

Melita's latest escapade of rebellion had damn near cost him his life. His daughter had to know that he wouldn't rest until he'd been compensated for that.

Downstairs he phoned Holic Reznik. "Give me an update. Is Merrick on his way yet?"

"He flew to Rome."

"Why Rome and not Athens?"

"I don't know. From Rome he took a flight to Crete."

"And?"

There was a long pause.

"Don't tell me you lost him. Did he make you on the plane?"

"I don't know how he got out of that hotel in Iráklion without us seeing him."

"Idiots. He's a damn master of disguises, that's how. I warned you to expect anything, and overlook nothing."

"He never made me on the plane. I look damn good as a woman, better than I expected. I did find out that a boat was waiting for him in the harbor."

"How do you know that?"

"I always find a way to make people talk, you know that. Before the fisherman choked on his own blood he told me a man left the harbor around midnight in an expensive little speed-demon cruiser."

"How do you know it was him?"

"The fisherman said the old man was wobbling on a cane with two left feet, but that he had no need for the cane or the limp when he leapt on board and sent the cruiser out of the harbor at full throttle."

"That doesn't help me now."

"I have the name of the cruiser."

"Did the fisherman say if someone picked him up? Paxton?"

"No. The *Aldora* was empty when Merrick sailed her out of port."

"Find the cruiser, and find Merrick. I didn't fly to Washington for nothing. Do it, Holic. I hold you responsible for my daughter's escape from Despotiko. Redeem yourself, or I'll have no reason to keep you around. You've been a disappointment lately, and you know what I do to men who disappoint me."

"Father?"

Cyrus slid his phone into his pocket, then turned around to see his son wearing sweat-soaked fatigues and a muscle shirt. "Where have you been, Erik?"

"I took a morning run."

"Your mother asked me to talk to you. She's still asleep. Perhaps this would be a good time."

"She's on the college kick again?"

"If she asks, tell her we've talked and you're considering it. Now come and fill me in on your progress."

His son followed him onto the veranda. Once they were seated, Cyrus studied Erik. The workouts over the past year were paying off. It was even more than he'd hoped for. It appeared Erik was putting his heart and soul into his work.

"I looked over the file Kipler's been keeping on you. It's impressive."

"Kip says I'm a natural. I can nail my target eighteen out of twenty now."

Erik flexed his muscles, and Cyrus could see that Kipler had made good on his promise to turn his son into a fighting machine.

Erik was staring at the fresh scars on his father's chest. "What happened?"

"An encounter with Merrick."

"Did you kill him?"

Cyrus had shared certain secrets with Erik. One of those secrets had been his life as a betrayed Onyxx agent left for dead in Prague. "No. He's as good as I am at cheating death. But the opportunity will come again. That's why you need to continue to keep up with your training. I don't want you vulnerable should he show up someday unannounced."

That would never happen. He'd made sure of that, but Erik needed to stay focused.

He didn't intend to tell Erik about Melita's defection. He would eventually have to if he didn't get her back in a timely manner, but for now Callia and his son would believe Melita was safe at Lesvago with Simon.

Simon... He'd shared his eldest son's death with Erik some time ago—a little fuel to ignite his hatred of Merrick, but there was no reason for Callia to know. Erik had proven his loyalty by keeping the secret. His son was a pleasant surprise, and Cyrus was rarely surprised by anything.

Simon had been weak, a burden from the moment he'd been born. His headstrong daughter and albino son with a frail immune system had been blessed curses from the beginning.

Weak, ungrateful children were a father's worst nightmare. But Erik was loyal to the bone, and when the time came Erik would follow his father into hell without even blinking an eye. If only he had another just like him. Several. Still, one loyal son was better than none.

He reached over and squeezed Erik's shoulder. "I'd like to see for myself how well you're honing your survival skills. We leave for the island day after tomorrow."

Erik's eyes lit up. "What will we tell Mother?"

"That we're going fishing."

They shared a grin.

The sun was up when Merrick returned to the *Aldora*. He went below deck, and to his surprise he found Melita waiting for him. She looked up on hearing him come down the companionway. Johanna's picture was in her hand, and the question she asked a second later was as confusing as the look on her face.

"Sully never mentioned that you knew Callia. How do you know my stepmother?"

Merrick frowned. "Stepmother?"

"You knew my father remarried after he killed my real mother. I don't see Callia often, but I do think of her as my stepmother. She's very—"

"You're mistaken. That's a picture of Johanna."

"Your wife, Johanna?"

"That's the only Johanna I know. Yes, my wife."

"Sully told me that she died."

"Cyrus killed her," Merrick clarified. "She was twenty-six in that picture. It was taken a month before her death. Are you telling me there's a strong resemblance between Callia and my wife?"

Melita looked at the picture again. "No. This is my step-mother."

Merrick tried to make sense out of what she was saying. "You know your father had extensive plastic surgery on his face. If there's a close resemblance, then Callia must have had reconstructive surgery."

It was too bizarre to believe, but then he knew what Cyrus was capable of. After all, he'd had plastic surgery to clone Paavo Creon, their comrade. He'd gone so far as to have one of his fingers amputated to match Paavo's hand. Nothing was beyond Cyrus's twisted mind. It was an extreme concept, but Cyrus was an extremist in every facet of his life.

"I never considered that." Melita laid the photo on the table. "I can't imagine why anyone would agree to that, but knowing my father, she probably didn't have a choice. The likeness is uncanny. Sorry, if I—" She stopped in midsentence, then spun the picture toward Merrick and pointed to Johanna's raised hand, holding her hair back from her face.

"See this scar. Callia has one just like it. She told me how she got it. She was rescuing her cat."

Melita's claim hit Merrick in the solar plexus like a sledgehammer.

"His name was something like Jasper or…"

"Jinx?"

"That's it."

Merrick sat down at the table before his knees buckled. "Tell me the story, Melita."

She relayed the tale while Merrick's memory followed along. Johanna had needed eighteen stitches to close the wound. He'd wanted to kill that damn cat, but the silver Siamese wasn't just Johanna's pet. She had loved Jinx like a mother loves a child.

A glass of water materialized in front of him. The sound of his name and a hand on his arm jerked Merrick back.

"Should I get Sully?"

"No. Sit down."

She sat across from him, and they stared at each other for several seconds. Finally, she said, "Callia and Johanna are the same person, aren't they?"

"I saw her die."

"You were there?"

"No. I watched it on my computer in my office at Onyxx headquarters."

"Could it have been someone else?"

"No. It was Johanna." It wasn't possible that she could have survived the explosion, but as that thought came to him, so did another. "Cyrus is an explosives expert. The warehouse was leveled." He thought a minute. "Time delay. He rigged the explosion on a timer. She wasn't in the warehouse when it blew."

"Did you find a body?"

"No. The explosion was double-charged. After searching through the rubble, we found nothing."

"Then why did you think she was inside?"

"She was in that warehouse. I saw her strapped to a bed

with C4. The warehouse was one of ours. I'd been there many times. I found her car abandoned at the shopping mall where she told me she was going that day. She was gone." Merrick pointed to the picture. "That photo is almost twenty years old. You said Callia looks like this now?"

"Pretty close. A little older, but not much."

"Johanna would be forty-six now. How's that possible?"

"I don't know."

Merrick knew that Cyrus had remarried, but they had never been able to uncover any data on the woman. It was obvious now why that was. He said, "You've spent time with her. How is she?"

"Not much time. Every other year I was allowed a visit with Simon."

"And how did she seem?"

"I'm not sure what you're asking?"

"You know Cyrus, Melita. If he has my wife, then she's living with him against her will."

"I don't think so. He treats her like a queen. Like he…"

"Like he what?"

"Loves her."

Merrick snorted. "You of all people know he's incapable of that."

"I know, but he's different with her and Erik."

"Erik. Their son."

"Yes. My half brother."

Merrick also knew that Cyrus had another child. A boy. He could not wrap his mind around the idea that Johanna had given Cyrus a son. Not willingly, anyway. Not his Johanna.

"How does she treat him? Is she afraid of him."

"No. She seems…happy."

"Happy?" The words tasted like poison in his mouth.

"She told me once that my father gave her a reason to live again. That he was the center of her and Erik's world."

"And you never told her that your life as his daughter was a living hell?"

"No, and she never knew anything about my situation at Despotiko, either. Or any of the other horrible things. I knew the rules, and I played the game. We both know what happens when my father is crossed."

Melita had seen far more tragedy than anyone should at age twenty-four. Her brother Simon was dead because of Cyrus, and she had witnessed the man she once loved beaten to death on her father's orders. The guilt over Nemo's death had caused Melita to slit her wrists. Luckily, she hadn't died.

"What are you going to do?" she asked.

He wanted to say, *Get my wife back,* but that was ego and wounded pride talking. It sounded as if Johanna was exactly where she wanted to be. Which meant she'd been in on Cyrus's scheme to stage her death. There was no other explanation that made any sense.

"What else can you tell me about my wi—her? When did you see her last?"

"In Naxos about three months ago. She wasn't feeling well the day I arrived. She'd had another asthma attack and—"

"Asthma? She's ill?"

"She has acute asthma."

"Can you take me to the house in Naxos?"

"Yes. But they're not there anymore. The week I visited, Zeta was packing up the house."

"Who's Zeta?"

"The housekeeper. That's her title, but she's a nurse by trade. She looks after Callia when my father is away. Zeta and her daughter, Sonya, have lived with them for as long as I can remember. Although I didn't see Sonya when I visited last."

"What's Zeta's last name?"

"Poulos."

There was a noise overhead, then Sully came down the

companionway. He glanced at Melita, then Merrick. "What's wrong?"

"What's wrong," Merrick said, "is that I've been a blind fool. Johanna's alive." He pointed to the picture on the table, then stood. "Melita tells me that's Callia. That my wife is Mrs. Cyrus Krizova. I'll let her explain. I need some air."

Merrick didn't know how long he stood staring out to sea on the *Aldora's* deck. Time… He'd spent years living in a time warp. That place where Johanna had kept him sane. He didn't feel sane right now.

He pulled his phone from his pocket to call Sly McEwen.

"Are you in Amorgos with Sully?" Sly asked.

"I'm here. Listen, I just…" Merrick still couldn't believe what he was about to say. "I just…"

"Merrick?"

"I've learned something."

"Have you located Cyrus?"

"No. But… Johanna is alive, Sly."

There was dead air on the line, then Sly said, "Are you sure? Do you have proof? You know how Krizova likes to torment you. Maybe—"

"It didn't come from Cyrus. It came from Melita. I'm checking in, like I told you I would once I got here. I'll tell Sully to give you a call later."

"If Johanna's alive, I should rally the men and—"

"If I need you, I know where to find you."

"You all right?"

"I can't talk right now, Sly. Sully will call."

Merrick slipped the phone in his pocket. Johanna was alive. Alive all this time, living in Greece as Cyrus's wife. Happily, Melita had said, with her husband and son. Cyrus's son.

Merrick closed his eyes as that fateful day surfaced in his mind. They had made love that morning in the shower, and then he'd gone to work. She'd told him she was going shopping, and hours later in his office at headquarters, he'd gotten the e-mail. *I have a picture you'll want to see.*

It was an odd e-mail, but he'd been curious. When he retrieved the picture, he saw Johanna on a bed of steel with a charge of C4 strapped around her body. He'd had no idea that the minute the picture materialized on the screen by his own hand he had automatically started the timed explosives.

For three minutes he had stared at Johanna's terrified face before the screen went black. Then came the report that an explosion had leveled one of their warehouses in Crystal City, ten miles south of Onyxx headquarters.

"Merrick?"

He felt Sully's hand on his shoulder. "I can't imagine what you're feeling right now. I don't know what to say."

"Cyrus faked her death."

"It looks that way."

"Twenty years of believing she was dead, and now…" Merrick cleared his throat. "I called Sly. I told him you'd call him later and fill him in."

"Whatever you want. Ask it and it's yours. The men can be here in—"

"No. That would be a waste of manpower right now. We don't have any leads on where Cyrus is."

Minutes of silence dragged by. Finally, Sully said, "There could be a reasonable explanation for why she's with Cyrus."

"Reasonable?" Merrick expelled a cold laugh. "What would that be, Sully?"

"She could be a victim. One more in a long list."

"A *happy* victim? A victim who gives her abductor a son? No. She went with him willingly, and there's only one reason why she'd do that."

"You think she was having an affair with Krizova in Washington?"

"After he survived Prague, he resurfaced with a new face.

He wanted revenge on me because I was the one who had left him for dead. What better way than to take my wife. Yes, I think he set his sights on Johanna. We used to talk about our wives. He knew how I felt about her."

"You think he approached her and they started seeing each other."

"Johanna was acting secretive about something for weeks before she died. Make that *disappeared*. Now I know why." Merrick pulled the envelope from his pocket and shook out the ring and the small white card. "Cyrus left these with Sarah Finny to give to me. Sarah is—"

"The woman from the flower shop."

"Cyrus put roses on Johanna's grave before he left Washington, along with this note." He handed it to Sully.

"Game on. Your move." Sully looked up. "He really is a sick bastard."

"That note was meant to bring me back to Greece so I would lead him to Melita. He never expected me to learn the truth about Johanna. But now I know something he doesn't."

"So, now what? Where do we go from here?"

"There's no *we*. You're staying here with Melita. Don't let her out of your sight."

"Where are you going?"

"To clear my head. I'll be in touch."

Merrick left the cove with no destination in mind. Every beautiful memory of Johanna was now tainted by lies. As soon as he faced that ugly truth, he decided, he'd be thinking more clearly.

Chapter 3

Cyrus had been home two days when he sailed with Erik on a short fishing trip. Callia was on her way downstairs when she met Zeta on her way up, her dark eyes red from crying.

"What's wrong?"

"I've gotten some bad news."

Cyrus and Erik hadn't been gone two hours. Had something happened to them on the *Starina?*

"What news?"

Zeta glanced over her shoulder as Kipler walked past. "It's personal. Can I speak to you privately?"

"Of course. Come with me." Callia led the way back upstairs. Inside her bedroom with the door closed, she said, "What's happened?"

"The hospital in Naxos called. My daughter's been in an accident. The doctor says it's serious, and I need to come right away."

"I'm sorry." Callia hugged Zeta. "I'll tell Kipler and—"

Zeta pulled away. "No. He won't let me go. I'm never to leave you."

"This is an emergency."

Zeta shook her head. "I need to go without anyone knowing I've left."

"That's impossible. Kipler has his orders. We'll need his approval."

"He'll say no."

Callia thought a moment. "I'll tell him we're going into Kerkyra to do some shopping. One of the guards can drive us. You can slip away once we're in town and fly to Athens, then to Naxos. Once you're gone, there won't be much he can do about."

"It might work."

"Go get ready."

Callia changed clothes, then went to the small safe in the study where Cyrus left money for her to use as she wished. She was standing at the window when a knock came on the door. "Come in," she said.

"You wanted to see me Kiria Krizova?"

"I'm going into town with Zeta, Kipler. Could you have one of the guards drive us?"

"How soon do you want to leave?"

"Right away."

Kipler nodded, and within the hour Callia and Zeta arrived in Kerkyra. Callia told Endre, the seasoned guard that often drove her to town, that she wanted to go to the market square. As he waited near the car, she and Zeta strolled the market. It was busy and that was a good thing. They quickly got lost in the crowd, and slipped into a cab. Halfway to the airport, Callia noticed that Zeta's anxiety had escalated.

"I don't think I can do this alone, Callia. I didn't mention it before, but I'm afraid to fly."

"You'll do fine. Don't worry."

At the airport Zeta had a panic attack. She was shaking so badly Callia was afraid she would never be able to board the plane. "You have to do this, Zeta. For Sonya."

"Come with me?"

"You know I can't do that."

Zeta collapsed in a chair. "I'm sorry. I know you can't, but I don't think I can do this alone."

Callia glanced at her watch. The plane would leave the runway in a matter of minutes. She hurried to the counter. "I'd like to purchase another ticket to Athens, then one to Naxos, please." When she returned to Zeta, she said, "Come on. I'll take you to Naxos, then fly back once I get you to the hospital. Kipler is going to be furious, but I'll call him once I'm on my way back from Naxos."

"You will? You'll come with me?" Tears streaming down her cheeks, Zeta jumped up and threw her arms around Callia and hugged her. *"Efkharisto."*

"You don't need to thank me. Not after all the years you've been so good to me. Come on."

Zeta gripped Callia's hand, and together they left Kerkyra. They changed planes in Athens at 1:00 p.m. and thirty minutes later they landed in Hora, the largest coastal city in Naxos.

"There's a taxi." Zeta pointed.

Callia led the way. The cabdriver opened the back door for them, and once they were inside and he was behind the wheel, Johanna said, "The hospital, please."

"No *aposkeves?*" the driver asked.

"No luggage."

He pulled away from the curb, and the car quickly slipped through the airport congestion. Callia said, "I wish I had time to see Sonya, but my plane leaves in a half hour to return to Corfu." She squeezed Zeta's hand. "You have my phone number and the extra money I gave you?"

"Ne."

"Call me later and tell me how Sonya is. Tell her I'm praying for her recovery."

Zeta hugged Callia as the car pulled to a stop in front of the hospital. She got out of the cab, stood in the open door. "I'm sorry, Callia."

"There's nothing to be sorry about. Call me in a few hours. I'll be home by then."

Zeta nodded, then with tears streaming down her cheeks, she closed the door and walked away.

"Back to the *aerothromio*," Callia told the driver.

"The airport," he repeated. "*Amésos*. Right away. No problem."

On the ride back Callia noticed that they were taking a different route and the cabdriver was pushing the speed limit. *"Piyene pio sigha."*

The driver didn't slow down. She saw him pull his dark sunglasses off and toss them onto the seat. He ran his hand through his silver hair, and this time when he spoke his island accent was gone. The deep baritone voice sent a cold chill up her spine—the voice as recognizable as the piercing gray eyes that now stared at her in the mirror.

"Hello, Johanna. Or would you prefer I call you... Callia?"

She was two feet from him, and he could reach out and touch her. Merrick quelled the urge—the urge to turned around and wrap his hands around her neck.

From the moment Melita had told him Johanna was alive he hadn't allowed himself to believe it entirely. Not until now.

"I'll say one thing for your housekeeper, she knows how to follow instructions. Of course, I did give her incentive."

"Zeta knew? Where's Sonya?"

"The girl is waiting for her mother in the hospital lobby. I suppose you could say her accident was running into me. When I spoke to your housekeeper a few hours ago on the phone, I suggested that she take her daughter and disappear as quickly as possible once she'd delivered you to me. If she's smart she'll do it. Otherwise Cyrus will kill them both for betraying him."

"He would never hurt Zeta and Sonya."

Merrick glanced into the rearview mirror. Her delicate features were strained, her voice full of fear. A fear that was directed at him, not the threat of violence from Cyrus against the hired help.

He swung the taxi into a crowded parking lot at Hora's busiest seaport and killed the engine. When he looked into the mirror again, he found Johanna's fear still glaringly evident. Her anxiety had altered her breathing, and it reminded him that she was asthmatic.

"I always knew one day you would come," she said. "Cyrus said you never give up on a mission."

"What mission would that be?"

"I know it was you who tried to kill me in Washington. Cyrus told me everything."

Those beautiful hazel-green eyes were as accusing as the tone in her voice. Sharp and on the attack. Whatever game she was playing, he was about to change the rules.

"I'm going to get out while you stay put. Move your ass into the center of the seat." When she didn't move, he said, "Rule number one. Never piss off the man who holds your life in his hands."

She slid left a few inches, and he opened the car door, slipped his sunglasses back on, then climbed out. He was dressed in jeans and a white shirt, the sleeves rolled up in the island heat. He tossed the keys onto the front seat, then opened the back left door and climbed in next to her.

He remembered everything about her, even the way she smelled. He found it ironic that she hadn't changed even her perfume.

"Did you kill the taxi driver?"

"He's taking a nap in a hotel room." He took her purse from her, opened it and dumped it out in her lap—cell phone, wallet, one lipstick, asthma inhaler. The inhaler made him aware of the shortness of her breath. He glanced at her chest, her sunbaked cleavage as smooth as satin.

Another memory came blasting through his controlled anger and he looked away, pocketed her cell phone and opened her wallet. Money, a passport that claimed she was Callia Krizova, one picture—a group photo of her and Cyrus with a young boy, maybe sixteen. They looked very *happy*.

He handed her purse to her, kept her wallet. "Take the inhaler, that's all you'll need." Then he reached up and jerked the clip from her hair releasing the thick knot. When she reached up in protest, he noticed the marble-size diamond ring on her finger.

She dropped the lipstick into her purse, set it in the seat next to her and kept the inhaler.

"Did you file for a divorce?"

She looked up. "What?"

"You heard me. Did you divorce me?"

She shook her head.

"Then that ring on your finger doesn't belong there." Merrick pulled the small envelope from his pocket. "Give it to me."

She looked down at her hand, but she made no effort to take off Cyrus's rock.

"I could cut off your finger. Should I?"

She took off the ring. He opened his hand and she dropped it into his palm. He shook his ring out of the envelope—a two-karat emerald-cut diamond set on a white gold wedding band wrapped with more diamonds.

"Put it on."

"Where did you get that?"

"Put it on."

She took the ring and slid it onto her finger.

Merrick pulled the white card Cyrus had left at the cemetery from the envelope, then dropped his garish four-karat diamond inside and slid it into his pocket. He reached down inside his boot and came up with his Nightshade. When she saw the knife, she clutched her hands together as if anticipating losing her finger.

He had never once laid a hand on her, never hurt her in any way, and yet her fear of him was indisputable. He had more than one good reason to inflict pain on her, but that was Cyrus's MO, not his. Not that he wasn't angry enough to let his rage fly.

He did it now, raised his hand and drove the knife blade into the back of the driver's seat. She cried out and tried to scoot away from him.

"Keep your ass nailed down."

He saw her glance at the white card, silently mouth the words. *Game on. Your move.*

"What's that?" Her voice hollow and full of trepidation.

"A gift from Cyrus. He left this and your ring in Washington for me a few days ago."

"Washington?"

"Did he forget to mention it?"

She looked dumbfounded. Didn't answer.

Merrick took her wallet, slid the white card inside and tucked the wallet into the hole he had sliced in the leather seat. Then he opened the door and climbed out. "Get out."

"If you kill me, Cyrus will come after you. He'll—"

"I didn't come here to kill you, Johanna. I only learned that you were alive a couple of days ago."

"I don't understand."

"That makes two of us. I never expected you, of all people, would betray me. I'm usually a better judge of character. Now get your ass out of the car."

She slid out and leaned against the back quarter panel of the cab. "You're the one who tried to kill me, remember?"

"No more lies, Johanna. You helped Cyrus fake your death, then ran off with him."

"I didn't fake anything, and I ran to save my life from the men you sent to kill me."

"That's bull."

She jerked away from the car. "I was there. I heard every word. Those men were acting on your orders."

"I never sent anyone to kill you, Johanna. If I had wanted you dead, I would have done it myself. I could have blown your head off any day of the week. We shared a house for five years, remember? A house miles from the closest neighbor. I could have buried you in the backyard under a rosebush in broad daylight and no one would have been the wiser."

That comment rendered her speechless for a moment. "If you're not going to kill me, where are you taking me?"

"On a little boat trip."

Her eyes shifted to the blue water and the harbor crowded with boats riding the tide.

Her hesitation made him say, "Rule number two. Never forget rule number one."

He had no idea how close Cyrus was, and as much as he wanted to face the bastard, he wanted it on his terms. He motioned for her to start walking, and he followed three steps behind her down the pier where the *Aldora* waited. When they reached it, he said, "Get in and go below."

He followed her down the companionway, swung the door open to the stateroom and, when she walked inside, he didn't say another word, just pulled the door shut and locked her in.

As he headed back up the companionway he noticed his hands were shaking. For the first time in months he wanted a drink. If he had a bottle on board he would have broken rule number three: Never let your emotions navigate a mission. Getting stink-ass drunk wasn't on his agenda, and he didn't trust the man he might find at the bottom of a bottle. He'd never been an angry drunk, but there was always a first time for everything.

The morning he'd woke up at sea after leaving Amorgos, he'd gone over everything Melita had told him, and within an hour he'd arrived in Naxos on the hunt for Zeta Poulos's daughter. Melita had said that Sonya wasn't living in the house the last time she'd visited.

He'd used every resource available to track her down believing there was no reason why she would have changed her name. In the end he'd resorted to his old government assassin tricks to find her. It had taken him thirty-six hours.

Sonya was eighteen and enrolled in a private school in Hora. Dressed as a priest bringing bad news he had met with the girl. His roll as kidnapper came late that evening once he'd gotten her away from the school. She had been more than willing to go with him after he'd told her that her mother was on her deathbed.

The glitch came after he had Sonya on board the *Aldora*. He'd revealed to her that her mother was very much alive and well, and what he wanted from her was the location of Krizova's most recent hideout. But the girl didn't know where Cyrus had moved his family after leaving Naxos—it was part of her agreement to be allowed to stay in Hora and go to school.

He'd told her that was unfortunate for her and, afraid for her life, she'd offered him a phone number where she could reach her mother in case of an emergency.

This was definitely an emergency, he had told her—a life-sustaining emergency, and she wouldn't want to end up at the bottom of the sea.

Moments later Sonya called her mother. On speakerphone Merrick had waited for the concerned mother to take a breath, then he'd taken over the conversation, giving Zeta Poulos explicit instructions—her daughter would die by three o'clock if she didn't follow them to the letter.

It was two o'clock when the plane from Athens had landed at Hora's airport. Merrick had watched the passengers exit the plane. It was the first time in almost twenty years that he had seen Johanna, but he spotted her easily. She wore white pants and a green satin blouse, her hair, still as long as he remembered, twisted in a sexy knot.

He'd stood numb beside the taxi, his dark sunglasses shielding his eyes as she guided her housekeeper toward him. Melita was right. Johanna's years in Greece had been kind to her. She looked far younger than forty-six.

Merrick climbed into the cockpit, and with a clear sky overhead and a million miles of azure sea to get lost in, the _Aldora_ sped away from Hora recklessly.

It was his silver hair that signified the passing of time, but it was the handsome face and amazingly fit body, his voice and those penetrating gray eyes that had turned back the clock.

She should hate him. Most days she had convinced herself that she did. But that was a lie. What she hated most was that she didn't hate him, and seeing him again only confirmed what a fool she still was.

She'd spent years in exile, hiding out like a criminal because of him. She had chosen a new life, or perhaps it had chosen her, but the memories of the old days with Adolf Merrick had continued to haunt her. They had spent five years together and she still couldn't forget how happy she had been.

Curled up on the berth in the stateroom, Johanna forced herself to relive that day so long ago. In the beginning all she had wanted was for it to have been some kind of horrible mistake. For days she had rejected the idea that Adolf wanted her dead. Night after night she had prayed he would come for her. That he would explain it all away, but it had never happened.

Forced to accept Cyrus's truth, her prayer had changed. She had prayed she would never see Adolf again and that the memories would die, as he had wanted her to die.

Please, God, kill the memories, and let me wake up hating him.

But God hadn't been merciful. The memories were branded in her mind with visions of what might have been. And now he was here, reminding her of all the pain she'd lived through. He was here tearing her heart apart for the second time.

Unwilling to surrender to emotional suicide, Johanna wondered what the significance was behind the white card. Adolf said Cyrus had been in Washington a few days ago. She wanted to refute that, but she had recognized Cyrus's handwriting on the card. At least it had looked like his.

Game on. Your move.

What did that mean?

She glanced down at the ring on her finger. The only person Adolf could have gotten the ring from was Cyrus. She'd worn it for weeks after her flight from Washington. The night she'd decided to take it off she was sitting on a veranda in Athens. Cyrus had come to sit with her, and after a long drought of silence, he'd said, "That ring on your finger belittles your intelligence. Why suffer the sight of Merrick's betrayal any longer? Give me the ring and I'll get rid of it."

Had he sent the ring back to Adolf long ago, or was Adolf telling her the truth? Had Cyrus been in Washington days ago?

It made no sense for him to bait Merrick. They had been living in hiding for years to keep from being discovered. It would be like calling up the devil and inviting him to tea.

So who did she believe? The husband who had betrayed her years ago, or the husband who had kept her safe for twenty years?

Johanna heard the cruiser's engine back off. She climbed off the berth and looked out the window. What she saw sent a cold chill up her spine—a crescent-shaped cove caged in by jagged rocks.

She had the answer to her question. Adolf was lying. This was where he was going to kill her.

A storm at sea hadn't been part of Merrick's plan, but as he skirted the southern tip of Rhodes it was evident that one was brewing. Buffeted against the wind, he dropped anchor in the cove and went below deck. For the next two hours he worked at the table on the second stage of his plan and, when he was finished, he held the ring up to the light and smiled.

"Game on, Cyrus. I made my move, and now it'll be your turn very soon."

The ring back in his pocket, he debated calling Sully but quickly dismissed the idea. He sat at the table and stared at the door to the stateroom for another hour, then stood and unlocked it.

He found Johanna curled up on the berth, her long hair shielding her face, her inhaler next to her. He glanced around the room. She had rifled through his belongings. He'd slipped the picture of her into one of the drawers beneath the berth. It was now on the floor, and he bent down, picked it up and slipped it into his back pocket like a kid guarding his favorite baseball card.

"Wake up," he said.

She stirred from sleep and sat up, sweeping her hair out of those beautiful eyes. She scooted back into the berth.

No, he needed her alive to make his plan work.

"Are you going to kill me now?"

"If that was the goal I would have popped you in the taxi, along with your housekeeper. Instead I bought her two tickets out of Greece."

"So you say."

"Where's Cyrus?"

"I'm not going to play your game, Adolf."

"Why not? You've been playing his for years. How long were you screwing him before the two of you decided to run off together?"

She looked confused. "I don't know what you're talking about. I met Cyrus the day you gave the order to have me kidnapped from my car and killed in that warehouse. Your men drugged me, and when I woke up I was bound with explosives strapped to some kind of steel slab. Cyrus found me before the explosives were set to go off."

"He just happened by at the right moment?" Merrick laughed. "They say timing is everything, but that's a bit hard to swallow, honey."

"I don't care what you think. I know what happened. Cyrus saved my life."

"So he's your hero."

"I'm alive because of him."

"What reason did he give you that I wanted you dead?"

"Onyxx business. A conspiracy you believed I was involved in?"

"What conspiracy?"

"He told me that my boss at the art gallery was a Russian spy. That you'd been onto him for years. That's why you married me. That you'd found evidence that I was working with him."

"Were you ever working as a spy?"

"No."

"Then how could I have found evidence that you were? There was no conspiracy, Johanna. If you were abducted, it was Cyrus who ordered it, not me."

"You're lying."

She seemed so damn sure about what had happened. Adamant that he had tried to kill her. Had she met Cyrus for the first time in the warehouse? Suddenly he knew it was true. She was speaking the truth. At least her version of what she believed happened.

"I overheard those men talking when I came to in the warehouse. They were talking about how you wanted me to die."

"They were Cyrus's men, not mine. He's an international criminal, Johanna. A rogue agent from Onyxx. He had you kidnapped and put in that warehouse."

"No! It was you," she screamed at him. "You wanted me dead. Go to hell, Adolf, and take your lies with you!"

"I've spent years in hell, Johanna. It's familiar territory." He reached out and pulled her off the berth and roughly hauled her to her feet. She cried out, and he let go of her before he could do something he would regret. "That you would think I could kill you is—"

"You're no saint… Icis. That's right. I know all about your days as an assassin. That part of your life you neglected to mention when you married me." She had climbed back on the berth and wrapped her arms around herself. "I saw your file. Before Onyxx you were a hired killer."

"It's true, I was a government assassin. A mercenary for hire before that. Cyrus used that information to cast doubt so you would believe him, Johanna. He used you."

"No."

"Yes, and you doubled his reward by climbing into bed with him and giving him a son. That must have made him laugh all the harder."

"You have no idea what you're talking about."

Merrick pulled his phone from his pocket. He'd downloaded the e-mail he'd received years ago from Cyrus. He hit the keypad then grabbed her hand and placed the phone in it. "Take a look, Johanna. That's what Cyrus sent me the day you disappeared…shopping. The day he let me believe he had killed you. That and four little words. *Game on. Your move.* I watched my wife die on a computer screen, and for twenty years until two days ago, I believed it was true. He did that. Your hero did that!"

Chapter 4

Cyrus got the call on the island. He'd just finished running Erik through a tactical course that would have killed him a year ago. He pulled his phone from his fatigues and saw that it was Kipler.

"What is it? I told you I didn't want to be interrupted. It better be a life-altering problem or—"

"They're gone."

"Who's gone?"

"Callia and Zeta. One of the guards took them to Kerkyra and they never returned to the car."

Cyrus glanced at Erik, then walked far enough away to keep from being overheard. "What the hell do you mean they never returned to the car?"

"They were shopping at the market square. When they didn't come back to the car after two hours, Endre went searching for them. He called me after he couldn't find them. I've sent the men out to search the town, but they're not having any luck."

"What time did they leave the house?"

"Midmorning."

Cyrus checked his watch. That was six hours ago. "Search again. Find her before I get back, or you will wish you had never been born." Cyrus slipped his phone back into his pocket, then turned to Erik. "We must return home immediately."

"Is something wrong?"

Cyrus didn't want to alarm his son, but he couldn't avoid the fact that somehow his men had misplaced Callia. "I'm sure there's an explanation for it, but it seems Kipler can't find your mother and Zeta. Did she mention that she intended to go into town and what she would be doing there?"

"No. But she did tell me about some things she saw for the house at the market square a week ago."

"Your mother had an asthma attack a few days ago."

Erik nodded. "A bad one. She had to use her nebulizer. She spent two days in bed."

Back on the *Starina,* Cyrus considered what could have happened. If Callia had surrendered to another asthma attack and it had been life threatening Zeta would know what to do. He didn't fear losing her to asthma; he'd taken every precaution. Still, he called Kipler back and told him to check the hospital.

But as he hung up he had to face another possibility. Merrick was in Greece, and as of yet Holic hadn't been able to find him or the *Aldora.*

Cyrus pointed the yacht north and headed back to Corfu, a slow rage building inside him. An uncontrollable rage that would have to be assuaged.

Endre was a dead man.

Johanna couldn't stop staring at the small screen on Adolf's phone, even though a band of pain squeezed her chest, slowly constricting her air.

She seldom had an asthma attack brought on by anxiety,

but she was still battling back from the attack she'd had days ago. She started to cough, a telltale sign that soon she would be fighting for her life, and still her thoughts raced on.

Merrick wants you dead. Come with me, Johanna. There's no time. We have to run.

Cyrus used you. I didn't know you were alive until two days ago.

Game on. Your move.

She slid to the floor staring at the ring on her finger. More coughing. Rapid panting. Dizzy.

"Johanna?"

Cyrus is an international criminal. A rogue agent. You doubled his reward by climbing into his bed and giving him a son.

"Johanna!"

Suddenly Adolf grabbed her and tried to force her inhaler into her hand. Johanna pushed it away. "Empty," she choked out. "Fresh air."

She heard Adolf swear, saw the inhaler land on the floor, then he was lifting her into his arms and hurrying up the companionway at a frenzied pace.

On the deck, he said, "Breathe, dammit. Breathe, Johanna."

He hadn't put her down, and his strong arms were wrapped firmly around her. She tried to focus, tried to concentrate on slow, even breaths, but she knew it would take her longer than a few minutes to regain her air. That is if she could do it at all.

Don't pass out, she warned herself. *Relax.*

"Come on, Johanna, take another breath. What the hell are you waiting for?"

She shoved at his chest, struggled against him. "Down," she croaked, the word so soft it was barely audible.

If he heard her, he chose to ignore her. He was hindering

her concentration. The feel of him, his voice, the familiar masculine scent—no cologne, just him.

"Johanna?"

"Put...me...down," she said in another weak attempt to get away from him.

Finally he was listening. He kept one arm around her waist as he set her on her feet. The air had turned chilly, the wind blowing hard. It sent her hair away from her face in all directions as the *Aldora* pitched and rocked against the gale that would soon result in rain.

Adolf's arm tightened around her as the boat rode out a four-foot wave that threatened to send the yacht crashing into the rocks. He pulled her back into his hard chest, his feet firmly planted.

Don't think about him, she told herself, just breathe. Relax and breathe.

When her lungs began to fill slowly with air, the wind seemed to subside with the end of her crisis, and the *Aldora* steadied herself. Still Adolf never let go of her.

Finally he asked, "How long have you been asthmatic?"

"Years," she said.

She'd contracted a lung infection weeks before Erik had been born. There had been no guarantee the medication wouldn't harm her baby so she'd refused it until Erik had been safely delivered. During that time the infection had done irreversible damage.

She turned in his arms and stared into those winter-gray eyes. "Let go."

He dropped his arm from around her and took a step back. "You said the inhaler is empty?"

"Yes."

"Why the hell would you go anywhere without adequate supplies for your health condition?"

"Maybe I was more concerned about Zeta and her daughter's *accident* than how full my inhaler was."

"Can you survive without it?"

"I just did."

"And if you couldn't arrest it?" When she didn't answer, he swore crudely.

She considered all the times Cyrus had reminded her of Adolf's intent to kill her. Moments ago he could have let her die, but he hadn't. And by the lingering concern on his face, even though he was angry she knew it was the furthest thing from his mind.

It was true. Her life since she'd left Washington had all been a lie.

"Why did this happen?" she asked.

"Why did what happen?"

"This. My life ripped apart."

"So you finally believe me?"

"Tell me why."

"And chance another asthma attack? I don't think you're up to hearing more tonight."

"You owe me an explanation. Now!"

He locked eyes with her again. "Revenge. Cyrus wanted revenge on me."

"So he steals your wife! That's some revenge."

"Remember the Prague mission?"

"Your weeks in the hospital afterwards. You were always reluctant to share details about your assignments. You told me it was to protect me. Perhaps if I had known more this wouldn't have happened."

"Cyrus was part of that mission. Our team walked into a minefield. A couple of the men lost their lives. Cyrus was badly injured. We were miles from nowhere. He wasn't going to make it, and I had wounded men depending on me to get them out alive. I left him behind. Somehow he survived, and when he surfaced he was a changed man, out for revenge."

"The scars on his chest…" Johanna recalled how Cyrus

had explained them. "He said they were from some betrayal. He was talking about you, wasn't he?"

"Your breathing is off again. That's enough for now. Next time fresh air might not be enough."

Later she would cry over the injustice of it all, but right now she was filled with rage. She stepped back and raised her hand. He saw it coming, but he didn't deflect her open-handed blow when it made contact with his cheek.

"This is your fault. How could you let this happen? Damn you, Adolf. Damn you!"

Merrick watched Johanna disappear down the companionway. She was right. It was his fault. All of it.

The guilt overwhelmed him, the pain in her eyes ripped his heart out. He gripped the railing, realizing now that she hadn't left him willingly. She'd run to save her life, she'd said. That she had lived all these years believing he had wanted her dead. That he'd ordered her death.

So much senseless pain. So many years swallowed up by lies with no way to eradicate the damage.

Merrick stayed on deck even after his tears had dried, and the anger returned. The sun had set, and a band of restless clouds brought the rain. It should have driven him below, but he remained on deck.

An hour later, he went below, soaked to the bone. peeling off his shirt as he passed through the galley and into the stateroom. Johanna was coming out of the bathroom. She was wrapped in a towel, and her hair was as wet as his.

On seeing him, she clutched the towel close. "Get out."

"I need some dry clothes."

He went to one of the drawers below the berth and grabbed underwear and a pair of jeans. When he turned, she was still clutching her towel.

"I'll be out of here as soon as I change." He ducked into

the bathroom and closed the door. He was back in a minute, a towel in his hand, drying off his chest.

She hadn't moved. As he began to towel-dry his hair, he saw her looking at it.

"You were always so dark. The gray hair is…"

He lowered the towel. "Is what?"

"Nothing."

"It's been twenty years," he said. "The irony in that is you don't look a helluva lot different. Cosmetic surgery? Cyrus should know where to find the best surgeon in the country."

"What's that suppose to mean?"

"After Prague Cyrus changed his face. He had several plastic surgeries to make himself look like another agent from Onyxx, then he killed him."

She looked away, turned back and raised her chin. "Perhaps it's the fugitive lifestyle that agrees with me. Or being pampered by lies, and deceived by a rogue agent with another man's face, out for revenge on my husb—"

"Husband?"

"Not for long."

She had a right to be angry, but dammit, so did he.

He tried not to notice how short the towel was, or how it hugged her ass. Tried unsuccessfully. He knew every inch of her body. He'd dreamed of her so often he could envision every curve beneath that damn towel. The rosy blush of her nipples, down to the soft, dark hair at the apex of her thighs.

It should repulse him to know that Cyrus knew every inch of her, too. It should, but in that moment all he wanted to do was pick her up and claim his wife.

She turned and reached for her pale green panties off her clothes pile on the berth. "If you don't mind, I'm going to get dressed."

"I don't mind."

She looked over her bare shoulder. "I'm asking you to leave."

He'd imagined her naked a million times in his dreams. He said, "I'll stay."

"Why?"

"To appreciate and remember."

She spun around. "Your memory is outdated, Adolf. It's as gray as you are."

With her back to him once more she opened the towel and let it drop. Her bare back was flawless, her ass as smooth and as sexy as the day he'd married her. He didn't blink as she stepped into her panties, then reached for her bra. When her fingers hooked it behind her back, he recalled the countless times he'd done that for her. Afterward she would turn in his arms and press herself against him, her hands slipping around him to fondle his ass. She would say something then, some little cock-teaser. She'd been a consummate flirt, and her boldness in the bedroom had kept him in a primed state of—

"Enjoying the show?" She had turned around, her blouse still open, as she ran the zipper of her white pants up her tan stomach.

Her phone went off in his pocket. He pulled it out, saw that it was Cyrus. "Hubby number two is looking for you."

She held out her hand. "Let me speak to him."

"And say what?"

"That Callia is dead, and that Johanna is alive."

"Bad idea."

"Why?"

"Right now what do you want most, Johanna?"

"I don't want anything from him, or you. Nothing but my freedom."

"Are you sure?"

She caught his eyes drifting to her breasts. She started buttoning her blouse. "If you think this ring means anything to me, you're wrong."

"That's not what I'm talking about. I imagine you'd like to see your son again."

"What the hell does that mean?" Johanna stalked after Adolf as he went through the door into the galley. "What about Erik?"

He turned on the light over the stove. "Telling Cyrus that you know the truth would be the biggest mistake you could make right now."

"My son belongs with me."

He turned and leaned against the counter. "Will he see it that way?"

That question made her pause. Much quieter, she said, "I want my son, Adolf."

"By now Cyrus has already suspected that I had something to do with your disappearance. Until we know what he intends to do about that, we're going to be silent and invisible. Who does the kid like better? Mommy or daddy?"

Johanna glared at him.

"Daddy?"

"Why does it matter?"

"Because if Cyrus learns you know the truth, then he's going to use Erik against you. That's what he does. He plays games to get what he wants."

"Erik would never believe a single lie about me."

"You believed the lies Cyrus told you about me."

Johanna felt the sting of his words. "So how do I get my son back?"

"I don't know yet, but I'll work on it."

He didn't sound as if it was going to be a top priority. "You'll work on it?"

"You're going to have to trust me."

"You had my trust once, and look where it got me."

He thrust her cell phone toward her. "Then call Cyrus and tell him you know the truth and see how far it gets you."

She stared at the phone, considered her options. "I won't call him, but you have to promise me that you'll do whatever it takes to free Erik from Cyrus. You owe me that."

"You're right. I owe you that."

* * *

Merrick turned and started to make himself a cup of instant coffee. Johanna wondered why. The coffeemaker was in plain sight, the small kitchen complete with all the amenities of a convenience apartment.

She watched him stir the brown crystals into cold water. *Cold water?* Watched him put it in the microwave for four minutes.

Give the man a gun and a tactical mission and he was in his element. Put him in the kitchen with a simple task and he became a danger to himself, as well as the kitchen.

He'd never been able to cook. It appeared he still couldn't even boil water. That made her curious about who had been taking care of him all this time.

Who had replaced her in his life? She shouldn't care. She shouldn't give a damn if he had a harem living with him.

"Do you want coffee?"

"What did you say?"

"Coffee?"

"No."

She glanced at the microwave, which had just shut off. He opened the door and her gaze moved slowly down his ruggedly fit body, lingered on his ass, still far too appealing for a gray-haired man over fifty. Unexpectedly, like a tidal wave, all the memories came rushing back. Memories of touching him and never getting enough of him.

"Son of a bitch! Too hot."

He'd burned his hand on the cup. "One and a half minutes."

"What?"

"The coffee. One and a half minutes. Did you see Cyrus in Washington?"

He left the cup sitting in the microwave with the door open. "No."

"Then how do you know he was there?"

"He was there. I got a description of him. He left that note with the Medallions."

"Medallion roses?"

"That's right."

"At our house?"

"No, at the cemetery."

"Why the…" Johanna frowned. Thought a moment. "That's right, I'm dead. He went to my grave and left roses? That's sick."

"I don't think you understand what motivates Cyrus."

"I'm beginning to."

"Before he left Washington he killed a man, and left two dozen Medallions at your grave with the note, and your ring with…a friend of mine to give to me."

Johanna hugged herself. "And after telling me all this, you think I'm going to wait around while you come up with a plan to get Erik away from him?"

"Yes. I'm trying to make you understand what Cyrus is capable of. He put Simon's life in danger countless times, Johanna. Simon died, caught in the cross fire of his father's revenge."

"Simon's not dead. I would know if—"

"You know only what Cyrus tells you, and that's based on what will keep you under his thumb."

You spoil me.

A spoilt wife is content.

"Eggs?"

"How can you eat right now?"

"Because I haven't eaten in two days, and eggs are something I can't screw up too badly."

"Simon is at Lesvago."

"No, his ashes are in the Aegean Sea. I know because I watched them being put in a jar before I sent them with Sully Paxton to give to Melita."

"Melita? You've talked to her?"

"Six weeks ago one of my agents stumbled upon her in one of Cyrus's compounds on Despotiko. Sully Paxton was being moved from one prison to another on Cyrus's orders. He's got hideouts scattered all over the islands. We raided the compound weeks ago and rescued two dozen men. Some were so emaciated they didn't survive. We also confiscated a cache of guns Cyrus was planning to sell to a band of global terrorists."

Johanna turned away and gripped the back of the semicircular booth that separated the galley from a small sitting lounge. It just kept getting worse. She felt sick, and she didn't want to hear any more, but she had to know. Know everything.

"What about Melita?"

"Melita was sent to Despotiko for falling in love with one of Cyrus's guards. Sully took her with him when he escaped the island."

"I saw Melita a few months ago. Cyrus brought her for a visit. She looked fine, and she never—"

"She seemed fine to you because she's smart, and she follows the rules. A wrong move and Cyrus would punish her. Have you seen the scars on her wrists?"

Johanna turned around. "What scars?"

"She slit her wrists after Cyrus killed the guard. Actually, he made Simon beat the man to death. Melita said you were getting ready to move again when she was there. Ever wonder why Cyrus insisted on moving you so often?"

"To keep you from finding us. I told you he convinced me that you would kill me if you ever found me."

"Common ground strengthens loyalty. Sacrifice, too. I'll bet you were damn grateful to him for all that protection."

It was true. "Where is Melita now?"

"Safe."

"Safe where?"

"Melita's survived hell. When this is over, and if you want to see her, I'll arrange it, but not before."

Over…

She wanted that, but she was afraid it would never be over. Not for Erik. He'd changed in the past year. He'd become more and more like Cyrus. That sent a new fear coursing through Johanna's veins. A fear that her son would never willingly leave his father, even if he knew the truth.

It was her truth, not his. Erik loved his father.

No, he worshipped him.

Chapter 5

Merrick cracked six eggs into the pan on the small stove. Over easy wasn't an option. It's how he liked them, but they always ended up scrambled. He quickly stirred the eggs into liquid and hoped for the best. Reached for the coffee in the microwave. Sipped the black brew that tasted scorched.

He put the spatula down. Let the eggs go, resigned to eat them no matter how they tasted or what color they were. He turned and leaned against the counter. "So now you know the truth. Care to share anything?"

She shook her head. "I want to see Melita."

"Still questioning whether I'm telling the truth?"

"No. I just want to tell her how sorry I am. That I didn't know what was going on."

"She feels the same way. She was as surprised as I was to learn that Callia and Johanna were one and the same. We actually found out together. That picture of you in the garden was what triggered it. Lucky I brought it along."

"Why did you?"

"Habit."

"That's not an answer."

The eggs were beginning to smell. Merrick turned back and picked up the spatula. They were already too dark. Shit.

"What did you mean, *habit?*"

"It's not important. Maybe you can talk to Melita tomorrow on the phone. I need to call Sully and give him the facts."

"The facts?"

He glanced at her. "After I learned you were alive, there were questions about exactly why you had run off with Cyrus."

"I know what you thought. Your exact words were, 'How long have you been screwing him?' You thought I was having an affair with him before I left Washington."

"Look, Johanna—"

She held up her hand. "So I was a conniving bitch having an adulterous affair, and then ran off with my lover."

The hurt in her eyes jabbed him with more guilt, and although it was what he had thought, Merrick said, "It was one scenario, but not the only one."

"It topped the list. Admit it."

"You have a right to feel betrayed by me and Cyrus. You'll get no argument on that from me."

"Translation. It topped the list. So I have a right to feel betrayed, and what do you have a right to, Adolf?"

"I have a right to my revenge. To right the wrong."

"Spoken like a tough guy with too much pride and ego to give a damn about anyone but himself. I believe I've just spent the last twenty years with him."

He smelled the eggs and turned back to the stove. They were burning and he quickly turned off the stove. "I made enough for two."

"They smell yummy. I'll pass. I think they'll get stuck in my throat along with everything else you've fed me today."

Merrick stared at the eggs. "Is there any way to rescue these?"

"Only one. The garbage."

"Go sit down." Johanna tossed the eggs into the garbage and started over. "What is there to drink besides coffee?"

"Water."

He had slid into the compact blue-leather booth, and she turned to look at him. "Nothing else?"

"Nothing."

"Not even a bottle of Glen Moray? You must have been in a hurry when you stocked the galley."

"Sully stocked the galley, and he knows I don't drink anymore. I don't smoke, either."

Impossible, Johanna thought. He drank every day since she'd known him, and had smoked two packs a day. "What's the story behind that?"

While she waited for his answer, she flipped the eggs carefully, then found a plate in the cupboard.

"It got old."

Translation. He'd become an alcoholic. She slid four over-easy eggs onto the plate, added two slices of toast that she'd dropped into the toaster, then opened the fridge and found the bottle of Tabasco. She brought the plate to the table. Set it down, then waved the Tabasco in front of his face. "Still like them spicy, or did that get old, too?"

"No, spicy is good."

She set the bottle on the table, and stared down at him.

He asked, "You going to join me?"

She hesitated, spotted the gold band on his finger. She slid into the booth. The wedding band looked like the one they had picked out together, but she couldn't be sure. It was just a simple wide band.

Had he remarried? It was obvious he hadn't spent much time in the kitchen. No doubt someone else was cooking for him.

"It's ours."

She looked up. "What?"

"The ring. I never took it off."

"Why not?"

He forked a healthy bite of over-easy eggs into his mouth. Chewed and swallowed. "Unlike you, I had no reason to. Where exactly in Corfu is home?"

"Two miles north of Kerkyra."

"Good strategic location?"

"The villa sits on a rock overlooking a three-sided bay."

"Like Lesvago."

"Not really."

"So you've been there?"

"Yes."

"What makes it different?"

"There's no long channel. The bay is open to the sea. Are you going after Erik?"

He finished his eggs. Sat back. "When the time is right."

"And when will that be?"

"I made my move. Now it's Cyrus's turn."

"This isn't a game."

"I hear the kid worships his father. That's what Melita said. Cyrus likes obedient children. The kid will be safe for now."

"How long are you going to wait? A few days from now? A week?" She shook her head when he didn't say anything. "I'm not going to wait weeks."

"First I get you out of Greece. Once you're safe, I'll—"

"There is no way I'm leaving Greece without Erik."

"You have no idea the force Cyrus is going to come at me with. And when that happens I don't want you anywhere near me."

"He's going to find that note in my wallet in Hora, isn't he?"

"He'll trace your flight pattern from Corfu. If he hasn't

already, I'll be surprised. Honestly, I wish I hadn't done that now, but—"

"You planned to use me to get him, didn't you? He used me against you, and you were going to do the same thing."

He slid out of the booth and stood. "Is Melita right?"

"Right about what?"

"He took you from me out of revenge. The question that hasn't been answered yet is why he kept you alive all these years. Or is there something you're leaving out? Did you crack Cyrus's cold heart? Does he love you?"

She slid out of the booth and faced him. "How should I know? I don't know him any better than I know you."

"What would your answer have been yesterday, Johanna?"

She tried to walk past him, but he snagged her around the waist and pulled her against him. "Does he love you?"

"Let me go, Adolf."

He held her a long moment and stared at her unblinking. "Or should I be asking, do you love him?"

"Let go!"

"I guess I have my answer."

"You have nothing."

"You're right. Cyrus made sure of that, didn't he? First he steals my wife. Then he steals her heart."

"Let go of me."

He didn't, just held on and stared at her. She looked away, feeling another wave of turbulent emotions battering her inside. Because she wouldn't surrender to them, wouldn't allow herself to be that vulnerable ever again, she said, "I slept with him three weeks after I left Washington, and I've been sleeping with him ever since. Is that what you wanted to hear? If I'm as good in bed as you always said I was, then perhaps I am worth keeping around."

The bitter reality of her words made him drop his hand. "Get some sleep. We pull anchor before dawn, and by noon tomorrow you'll be out of Greece."

"I'm not leaving without my son," she shouted as he turned his back and headed for the companionway. "I'm in the game now, Adolf. You put me here, and here I'll stay until I have my son back!"

Her words drove him back on deck. Merrick climbed into the cockpit and sat while the rain beat down and the wind whistled like a siren. But even over the noise, he couldn't block out Johanna's words.

After she had been taken from him, he had attempted suicide many times. He'd recklessly lived off cigarettes and Glen Morey for weeks after the funeral. More than once he'd passed out in a darkened alley, only to wake up disappointed that someone hadn't come along and slit his throat.

Day after day, night after night, it was the same hell. Haunted one minute by her image, and tortured the next by the reality that he would never see her again. Then the brain tumor came, and he'd thought, *Good, now I can escape hell on earth.* But as the weeks drifted into months, his hell turned into an obsession to find the man responsible. He'd made a commitment to Johanna to avenge her death, begun living inside the dreams—and suddenly the memories had become his saving grace.

The day he had divested himself of his imprudent habits, he'd gotten down on his knees and prayed that when it came time for brain surgery he would survive. That prayer had been answered, and he never touched a drink or a cigarette after that. But the one habit that he hadn't shaken was Johanna. And that was more than evident by the rampant emotions that he'd had to face the moment he'd laid eyes on her getting off that airplane. And every minute since he'd been straddling the fence between what he remembered and what he would never forget. The fact that Cyrus knew his wife as well as he did, perhaps better, was killing him.

Johanna was right, pride and ego were a man's biggest

enemies. But he couldn't let it go. Even now, after all she'd said to him, or maybe because of it, he was boiling beneath the surface.

Cyrus had ripped his heart out years ago, but tonight Johanna had sliced it into pieces. He supposed it was her right. He deserved everything she had tossed at him, but it still hurt like hell.

Johanna's phone rang again. He pulled it from his pocket and, after it stopped ringing, Cyrus left a message.

Callia, I'm worried, and so is Erik. Call me.

The galley was dark and empty when he went below. He entered the stateroom to find Johanna curled up on the berth. He realized the moment he saw her it was a mistake to think that he could sleep anywhere close to her. He turned and started back out the door.

"Where are you going?"

He turned back. "I just came to check on you," he lied.

"You're all wet again."

"I'll dry out."

"You asked for it."

"Asked for what?"

"My opinion on Cyrus's feelings."

"I think I got a little more than I was prepared to hear, but truth is truth."

"And now I'm a whore."

"I don't think that."

"Go away."

"Okay, three weeks seems a little soon, but you thought I tried to kill you, and—"

"Just shut up. You don't know what you're talking about."

"I'm trying to understand."

"You don't want to understand anything. All you see is that I betrayed you twenty years ago by leaving Washington with Cyrus, and then by sleeping with him. Go away and leave me alone."

She rolled over and gave him her back. The sheet had slid away and he saw she wasn't wearing her blouse. He focused on the smooth curve of her back, the pale-green bra straps.

"I don't want to fight, Johanna."

"Then you need to rethink your plan. If you send me away, I'll fight you every step of the way. I want my—"

"Kid. I know, I understand that."

She rolled back and sat up, the sheet falling to her waist. "You can't possibly understand unless you've raised a child. Have a few you've neglected to tell me about?"

"No. But that doesn't make me unsympathetic."

Her breathing was odd. Afraid to leave her alone, he unzipped his jeans.

"What are you doing?"

"Going to bed."

"Not in here." She lay back down, expecting him to leave.

"You're wheezing. Are you—"

"Having another attack? No. It's just how I breathe."

"I don't believe you." He debated leaving his jeans on, but they were wet. He dropped them to the floor and left them there. He didn't pull back the sheet, opting to sleep on top of it. He laid down on his back beside her, then reached up and turned off the small light on the wall and closed his eyes.

Several minutes ticked by, then she asked, "Do you have someone special in Washington? What am I saying? Of course you do."

"It's late. Go to sleep."

"That's a yes, right?"

"No."

"Then there's more than one?"

"No, as in, no one."

She rolled over, and he knew that she was staring at him in the dark.

"Go to sleep."

"You still wear the same kind of underwear, I see."

"It's dark. I doubt you can see anything."

"Still a size thirty-four?"

"Dammit, Johanna," Merrick opened his eyes and turned his head to find her elbow raised, propping her head. Her face was only inches away from his. "If this is some kind of ploy to get me to change my mind about getting you out of Greece, it won't work. In the morning you're gone, so quit this little seduction game and go to sleep. I'm not interested in screwing you."

She reached out and laid her hand on his crotch.

"What the—" He grabbed her hand. "Son of a bitch."

She twisted her hand free. "Feels like you're more than ready to screw something."

"Go to sleep."

"You never used to snore. Now that you're old and gray, do you?"

"Does Cyrus? He's older than I am."

"As a matter a fact, he does."

"Well, I don't. So you won't get confused in the middle of the night and forget who you're sleeping with."

He rolled over onto his side to get away from the smell of her skin. It was damn uncomfortable just to move. He had a hard-on that could drive a nail through an oak tree.

She stopped talking after that, and before long he heard her soft breathing, a sign she had fallen asleep. He rolled onto his back again, turned his head. She was curled up on her side in the way he remembered, her beautiful eyes closed, and her lips parted.

He lost track of time as he watched her sleep—time had no meaning since he'd found her. He stared and stared and stared until she rolled over and faced the wall. God took pity on him an hour later and he finally drifted off to sleep.

It was the first time in years he didn't dream. The first time that Johanna's ghost didn't pay him a visit. But then why would she? The ghost had become flesh and blood.

Sometime in the night, unaware, Merrick closed the distance and spooned her warm, soft curves.

In the morning Merrick woke up alone, the scent of Johanna on the pillow. He rose quickly, pulled on his jeans and stepped into the galley to the aroma of freshly brewed coffee.

Johanna was seated at the table eating a fried-egg sandwich. Next to her plate was her cell phone. She'd stolen it out of his pocket.

"What did you do, Johanna?"

Her answer came as she lifted a cup of coffee to her lips. "I've changed your mind for you."

"What the hell does that mean?"

"I called Cyrus and gave him our location."

"You don't know our location."

"I've been to practically every island in Greece. I recognized the shoreline yesterday when you brought me on deck. We're on the southern coast of Rhodes."

"So it was a lie? The story you fed me yesterday was all a lie."

"No. It happened the way I said it did. But then, it's your choice to believe me or not. I suppose it would make it easier for you to sleep at night if I was an adulterous whore, and a liar, too. By the way, how did you sleep? Remember much?"

"What does that mean?"

"Still a snuggler. I guess either you are or you're not. Cyrus isn't."

He had woke up on her side of the bed under the sheet. Last night he'd been so damn tired that once he'd fallen asleep he hadn't moved. Or had he?

"When I woke up I took time to check you over. Like I said, you sleep hard when you're tired. You still moan in your sleep when I touch you." She raised her hand, wiggled her ring finger. "Wifely rights. They are a size thirty-four, and the same black Jockeys I used to buy you." She glanced at his hair. "I'm still a bit in shock over the gray hair, but it fits you. It makes you even edgier than before. The scar on your temple, too. Though I'm guessing that's why you wear your hair a little longer than you used to. How did you get it?"

"I had my brain extracted," he growled at her. "That's the only excuse I have for giving you enough rope to hang yourself."

"Instead of standing there scowling at me, I'd pull anchor before Cyrus arrives and kills us both. He wasn't happy to hear that you demanded your husbandly rights last night."

"My what?"

"Okay, so I stretched the truth a bit, but since I'm in a position to know who's the better lover, I wasn't lying when I told him he falls a little short."

Merrick ran his hand over his stubbled jaw. "Do you have any idea what you've done?"

"I know exactly what I've done. Today you're going to be too busy staying one step ahead of Cyrus to think about sending me away. It really was a bad idea, anyway. Who's going to cook your eggs?" She held up her fried-egg sandwich. "Moist, with cheese, on lightly toasted bread. Pepper, and just a hint of salt."

Merrick could have strangled her in that moment. "What else did you tell him?"

"That was about it. I suppose I should take a shower." She turned her head and sniffed her shoulder. "I can smell you on me."

Merrick plowed his hand through his hair. "I never touched you."

"Are you sure?"

"Son of a bitch!" He snagged the phone off the table, pocketed it, then took the companionway three steps at a time. He barely noticed the sun was on the horizon, or that the sky was clear. He pulled anchor, then climbed into the cockpit and sent the *Aldora* out of the cove like a shot fired from a gun.

Chapter 6

The *Aldora*'s engine was in trouble. It had started out with a monotone hum, then a high-pitched ringing noise broke into a crescendo, like an opera singer belting out a final note. There was nothing after that, not even a squeak.

The *Aldora* reacted to the swan song as if she'd hit an invisible wall. Johanna stayed seated in the galley. Seconds later she heard Adolf's footsteps. He strode past her, giving her one quick, angry look, then swung open the door into the engine room.

"What's happened?" she asked, not getting up.

"Something's wrong with the engine."

She went to stand in the doorway of the engine room. Adolf was on his knees, going after the engine like a navy mechanic on the front line. He'd always been good at fixing things. How he'd learned so much about everything had always been a mystery, but she'd come to appreciate it. He could fix a blender, a lawn mower or rewire an electric outlet without giving it a second thought.

She was on her way into the stateroom when she heard him swear, then yell, "Johanna!"

Like a bolt of lightning he came after her, his anger scorching with a charred expression that could only be understood by someone who knew exactly what sabotaging an engine meant.

"What the hell were you thinking?"

She stared at him standing there with his jeans hugging his size-thirty-four waist, his bare chest as muscular as a man's half his age. She didn't believe for a minute that he hadn't been pursued in Washington over the years. There had to be some practice involved in being able to keep *it* hard all night.

"Why?"

"Why what?"

"Did Cyrus tell you to pull that oil plug?"

"No."

"You thought it up all on your own?" He shook his head. "I doubt that."

"Actually, I did."

"So Cyrus would catch up to us."

"I lied about talking to Cyrus. I never called him."

"And I would believe you after this?"

"You convinced me last night that it would put Erik at risk, and I would never do that."

"Then why the hell did you say you did?"

"So you'd overexert the engine in a fast getaway and burn it up. I told you, I'm not leaving Greece without my son."

He swore, turned and started to walk away.

"Adolf."

He turned back.

"There's something you should know."

"There's more?"

"One thing more. As committed as you are to Onyxx and your revenge, I'm twice as committed to my son. When you're ready to agree that my son is as important to me as your mission is to you, then we'll be on the same page."

"A helluva way to make your point."

"Then maybe next time you'll listen, instead of do all the talking. Isn't that the key to a good marriage? Hungry... honey? Want me to make you one of my fried-egg specials?"

"What I'd like to fry right now is your ass."

"Adolf!"

He stormed out the door, this time opting to stop talking and listening altogether.

For the rest of the afternoon Adolf ignored her. He was determined to fix the engine. He worked tirelessly, his language volatile and nasty. He swore the engine to hell, cursed himself, and before he started on her, Johanna took refuge on deck.

The sun was hot and all she could see was azure water in every direction. They were adrift in the Aegean Sea some-where between the Cyclades and the Dodecanese. The closest island looked miles away, a dirt speck in the distance.

The current kept them moving. Eventually a fishing boat would spot them and offer to tow them ashore. At least she hoped so. She wasn't a good swimmer and with her asthma it would be impossible to make it to one of the small islands if they were forced to abandon the yacht.

She rolled up the sleeves of her blouse and opened the top two buttons. She kept an eye out for a boat to come by, and as the hours passed, the idea of rescue before dark started to look unlikely. The current had taken them farther away from the island she'd spotted earlier. But it had been replaced by another one—still too far off to reach without a long, hard swim.

Just as the sun was setting, Adolf appeared on deck. His bare chest was covered in grease, as well as his jeans, and he smelled like gas and oil. He glanced at her, gave her a disgusted look, then pulled *his* phone from his pocket and disappeared inside the cockpit.

He was calling someone. No doubt Sully Paxton. Maybe he should have done that hours ago, instead of trying to salvage a dead piece of iron.

She wondered how far away his agent was. How long it would take for him to reach them, and how soon after that Adolf would send her away.

Johanna prayed he had changed his mind, but she knew that would take an act of God. But it wasn't God who changed Adolf's mind—a moment later he was scrambling out of the cockpit with a pair of binoculars.

He turned his back to her and began scanning the sea. She squinted, searched the growing darkness. She saw a faint light in the distance, then heard the sound of a boat. Maybe now they would be rescued.

"Is it a fishing boat?" she asked.

Adolf turned to her. "Get in the water and start swimming. Go now!"

The urgency in his voice told her that whoever was speeding toward them wasn't coming to rescue them. She said, "Is it Cyrus?"

"Get your ass in the water and start swimming for that island." Then he vanished below deck.

She dropped into the water and started to swim in the direction she remembered last seeing the island. Twenty yards from the boat, she stopped and looked back. Adolf was on deck again, a wicked-looking gun strapped to his bare chest, a coil of rope dangling from a wide belt hugging his waist, and a backpack on one shoulder.

He glanced at her. "Swim, dammit!"

Merrick caught up to Johanna within minutes. He could see that she was struggling to breathe. "Stop and catch your breath," he ordered.

When she did, she started to cough, and that sent fear racing through him. It made his concern sound like anger when he reached for the front of her pants, yanked her close and said, "Maybe after today you'll decide to listen to your husband."

"I don't have a husband." More coughing. "I've decided... two is two too many, and I'm... divorcing you both."

"Stop talking and focus on your breathing."

"What are you doing?"

"I'm tying you to me so you won't have to work so hard." He threaded the rope through her belt loop and tied it. "I'm going to lead out. When you feel the rope pull tight, start swimming. You won't have to exert as much energy."

"Is it Cyrus?"

"I can't be sure. But it's no fishing boat."

He took off, and in a matter of seconds he felt the rope tighten up. He glanced back once and saw Johanna was doing what he'd told her. He dug in then and moved through the water like a shark was on their asses.

Johanna was doing her best to keep up, but he worried that, even with some of the stress taken off her lungs, she would suffer an attack before they made it to the island. If that happened, he wasn't sure he would be able to save her.

The irony of that, of losing her a day after he had found her, was unacceptable. Merrick put everything he had into swimming faster, and as the shadow of the island drew near, and the cover of night became their ally, it looked like they were going to make it.

Minutes later the sudden burden of the rope told him that Johanna was in trouble. He slowed up and glanced back, but he didn't see her.

Sly McEwen had been waiting to hear news from Greece for four days. Although he'd been anxious as hell, it wasn't until that evening as he was leaving Onyxx headquarters that he had decided to call Merrick. But his commander didn't pick up.

He arrived at his apartment, ate supper with Eva, his fiancée, then tried Merrick again. Still nothing.

He hadn't told Eva much about Merrick's return to Greece. Cyrus Krizova was a hot topic, and it brought back the years Eva had spent in Cyrus's clutches as part of one of his revenge plots against her father, Paavo Creon.

Cyrus had killed Eva's mother, and eventually Paavo, too. The mere mention of Cyrus sent her down that black road.

"You're unusually sober tonight, Sly. Did something happen at work?"

Nothing had happened, that was the problem, Sly thought. "No, it's been quiet."

"That's good, right?"

She was curled up on the couch, her long red hair framing her beautiful face. She patted the space beside her and he sat down, stretched out his long legs and closed his eyes.

She snuggled against him. "You know I'm very good at being able to tell when something is bothering you. What is it? You get like this when… Is it Krizova? What has he done this time?"

"I don't want you to worry."

"Then be honest with me, Sly. We've been through a lot, and the reason it's working…us, is because we share everything. Don't we?"

"Cyrus was in Washington a few days ago." Her silence made him open his eyes. "He didn't come for you. He came for Briggs."

"Peter Briggs? Why?"

"Peter was Cyrus's mole at Onyxx."

"Was?"

"Cyrus flew in, killed him and left."

"Left? Now I know there's more to it than that."

"He left a few things behind for Merrick. Merrick's back in Greece."

"And you wanted to go with him."

"I did. We all did. Ash and Pierce, too. They've been calling me every day to see what I've heard."

"And?"

"And nothing."

She sat up. "There's more. What is it?"

"Merrick called me when he got there. It seems Johanna is alive."

"She's alive? How can that be? I thought—"

"We all thought she was dead. That explosion Cyrus set off was pretty convincing, but he faked her death, and took her with him. I talked to Sully and he confirmed that it's true. Merrick took off after he found out. There's been no word from him since."

"So call him."

"I did. He's not picking up."

"Then call Sully. Maybe he's heard from him."

"I was hoping he'd call me."

Eva sat up and reached for Sly's phone on the coffee table. As if it were her own, she popped it open, scrolled. "You have been promising that I could visit Melita. Maybe this would be a good time." She hit a button on the phone and handed it to him. "I'll start packing."

As she was leaving the room, Sly heard Sully's voice.

"What's up, big guy?"

"You hear from Merrick?"

"I did. Me and Melita are on our way to lend him a hand right now. Seems his cruiser's in distress and he needs rescuing. That's rich. Merrick needing rescuing."

Sully sounded upbeat. That was good. "I tried to call him. He's not answering."

"Probably too busy."

"Busy with what?"

"He's with Johanna. He found her yesterday."

"How did he manage that so damn quick?"

"He didn't give me details. I'll get them when I see him."

"What about Cyrus?"

"Merrick said he wants to get Johanna out of Greece. Once he does that, he's going after Johanna's kid."

"He's going to need us for that."

"He's still adamant that he's going to handle this his way."

"When you pick him up, tell him to give me a call."

"Will do. I'm an hour away from picking them up. Catch you later."

Sly tossed the phone on the coffee table. Merrick had already found Johanna. How in the hell had he managed that without running into Cyrus?

He didn't like it. Merrick going after Cyrus on his own. Maybe he was just feeling cheated. They had worked side by side for years to catch Cyrus. Yeah, that was it. He felt cheated.

"Eva, stop packing," he called out to her.

She stuck her head out of the bedroom. "Why?"

"Come sit down and I'll fill you in."

"It's the *Aldora*. Board her."

The call from Holic Reznik had come while Cyrus was combing the Cyclades Islands. Holic had said that they hadn't been able to keep up with Merrick's cruiser. That she had been heading south into the Dodecanese when he'd lost sight of the *Aldora*.

As four armed men went over the side of the *Starina*, Cyrus stood on deck. The Aldora was *adrift*, and he knew she'd been abandoned. He scanned the black water, waiting for the *Aldora* to be secured to the *Starina*, then he boarded her.

He went down the companionway, heard one of his men say, "She's empty. It looks like engine trouble."

Cyrus moved through the underbelly of the cruiser, his eyes missing nothing. He passed through the galley, glanced into the engine room. Confirmed what his guard had said—it was obvious Merrick had tried to repair the stalled engine.

"Wait for me on deck," he ordered.

As his men scurried up the companionway, Cyrus stepped into the stateroom. He saw Callia's inhaler on the floor and picked it up. She would never go anywhere without her inhaler, unless she left in a hurry, or... He checked it and found it was empty, then he glanced at the berth. He stepped closer, picked up one pillow and raised it to his nose. He didn't recognize the scent, but it was definitely masculine. He picked up the other pillow and sniffed it. The familiar erotic scent, a blend of roses and honey, lingered. Callia had slept in the berth. Slept next to Merrick. The question was, had she slept with him willingly, or by force?

He tossed the pillow on the floor. He returned to the deck and saw Erik at the *Starina's* railing, waiting for him. He dropped the empty inhaler into the sea and joined his son.

"What did you find, Father?"

"Merrick has your mother. Go to my stateroom and wait for me."

"But—"

"Go now, Erik." As his son left the deck, Cyrus locked eyes with Kipler. "Bring Endre's body up and toss it over the side onto the *Aldora,* then cut her loose and set her on fire."

The *Aldora* had just started to burn when Cyrus heard a boat coming hard and fast. A pair of night-vision binoculars confirmed that it was the *Korinna,* Sully Paxton's wicked bitch cruiser.

Fifty yards away, the boat turned away from the *Starina.* With the big yacht's two engines at full throttle the *Korinna* would be a challenge to catch. Cyrus swore, then he yelled to his captain, "Overtake her or you're dead!"

And the chase was on.

The size and speed at which the yacht had come out of nowhere had put Merrick on red alert. He'd been right to abandon the *Aldora*. He stood on the island shore and watched flames light up the sea and reach for the sky.

So the game *was* officially on. Cyrus had been to Hora and he'd found Johanna's wallet.

He hunched down by her where she sat on the beach against a rock. Her breathing was better. "How are you feeling?"

"Something's wrong."

"You swallowed water, and you're exhausted. Just rest."

"No. Something's wrong with my leg." She reached down and touched her thigh. "Ouch."

There were no stars out, no moon. It had given them the advantage in their escape, but now he could barely see the agony in Johanna's face. He reached for the backpack and pulled out his hot-spot flashlight. He wasn't too keen on turning it on and chancing being spotted on the open shore, but Johanna was in pain, and he needed to know why.

He turned on the light to examine her thigh. "Dammit. A sea urchin got you. I can see the spines through your pants."

It wasn't good, but at least he knew it wasn't a jellyfish, or Greece's poisonous weever fish. But the spines were going to have to come out, and it was going to be an uncomfortable ordeal.

With Johanna's asthma threatening to flare up at any time, she didn't need one more damn thing attacking her.

He was angry that he'd allowed this to happen to her. Angry that he hadn't taken the precautions necessary to ensure her safety. Taunting Cyrus had felt good, but it had been a mistake. One that Johanna had paid for today.

"Where are we?" she asked.

"I'm not sure. We drifted all day."

He turned off the light and stuck it back in his bag. He shouldered the bag, then picked up Johanna.

"Where are we going?"

"We need to get off the beach." He carried her fifty yards before he spotted a shallow cave. Inside, he laid her down.

"It was Cyrus, wasn't it?"

"It was Cyrus." Merrick pulled the hot-spot out of his pack, dug a hole in the sand, jammed it in, packed sand back around it and turned it on to light up the cave. "I need to get those spines out of your leg, Johanna. I don't want to chance driving them in any deeper, so I'm going to cut your pant leg open."

She tried to sit up to look at her leg.

It wasn't a pretty sight, and Merrick stopped her. "Stay on your back." Then he reassured her, "I guarantee your leg will match the other beauty again in a few days."

She closed her eyes, muttered, "You always liked my legs."

He pulled up his pant leg and jerked the Nightshade from the Kydex sheath inside his boot. The blade was as black as the moonless night and as deadly as a bullet. He dug through his tactical bag and retrieved his medical kit—it was a good thing he'd taken a few minutes to pack a few supplies before he'd abandoned the *Aldora*. He opened the medical kit and pulled out a loaded syringe.

"What's that?"

"Something to make you sleep while I'm removing the spines."

She eyed the needle. "I don't want to go to sleep."

"Just for a little while, honey. It's going to hurt like hell digging those spines out, Johanna. I'm not going to put you through that when I can make it easier on you."

"No! I don't want it."

"It's my call."

"It's my leg."

"You need to trust me."

"I do, but…"

"Then relax, and when you wake up, the spines will be gone."

She didn't fight him when he unbuttoned her blouse and jerked it past her shoulder. Then he gave her the needle, and while the drug took effect, Merrick cut her pants open from ankle to thigh, careful when he reached the area surrounding the spines.

After dark the islands always cooled off, and before morning it would get downright chilly. He didn't really want to make shorts out of her pants, but wet pants weren't going to do her much good, anyway. After he got rid of the spines he would get rid of as much wet material as he could. He didn't need Johanna getting sick on him on top of everything else she was going to have to deal with for the next couple of days.

She had lost her sandals in the water, which was going to make things even more difficult, but he would worry about one thing at a time.

He sterilized the Nightshade with alcohol from his medical kit, and once the drug had put her to sleep, he began working tirelessly, removing the spines one at a time.

She was right. He'd always liked her legs. He still did. And while he bandaged her thigh with a sterile dressing from his bag, he allowed himself the pleasure of touching her beautiful legs as he made shorts out of her pants.

She was wrapped in a blanket of heat. That was Johanna's first thought as she woke up from the drug that had knocked her out like a hammer to her head. She was on her side, and behind her she heard Adolf's steady breathing.

She slowly oriented herself and realized that the blanket of heat was warm flesh spooning her body.

Naked flesh.

The pillow behind her head was one of Adolf's arms, the other was wrapped around her waist, and his leg was curled over her hip.

They were all tangled up—and the memory it sparked brought her fully awake.

"Warm enough?"

He wasn't sleeping.

"Yes. Was I a good patient?"

"Spines are out and you'll be good as new in a few days."

"Did you save my life?"

"Sea urchin spines aren't fatal, just painful as hell. Speaking of pain. How's the leg feel?"

"It's fine."

"Details."

"It feels warm and stiff."

He said nothing, and she quickly felt something else warm and stiff shift away from her backside as he lifted his leg off her hip, careful not to bump her thigh.

"You were wet and shaking, and the night air wasn't helping. I decided I'd share my built-in heater with you."

It was dark in the cave. He must have turned off his flashlight to save the batteries. She rolled onto her back and angled her head so she could see him. She couldn't—it was too dark. "That was unselfish of you."

"You think?"

The tone in his voice suggested he was smiling. He moved and she knew he'd sat up.

"Our clothes are drying out on a rock. I would have taken off the rest of yours if I could have managed to get your pants off without hurting your leg."

She guided her hand over her pants to where he'd cut them off. "These are not pants," she said. "Get them short enough?"

"You can blame that on the sea urchin, not me."

She glanced toward the mouth of the cave, realizing the peril of their situation. "I'm sorry I sabotaged the *Aldora*."

"It's done. Now we go on from here."

"When?"

"It's not dawn yet. You should sleep a while longer, and then we'll see how your leg feels."

"Are you going to sleep?"

"I'll sleep later."

"You think Cyrus is close, don't you?"

"No. After he torched the cruiser, I heard a boat. The *Starina* took chase. I figure he went after Sully Paxton."

"Sully?"

"I called him to pick us up after I couldn't fix the engine. Cyrus showed up before he could get to us. He probably recognized Sully's cruiser and that's why he went after it."

"Are you worried that Cyrus might have caught him?"

"No. The *Korinna* isn't only fast, Mad Dog Paxton lives for speed. He can outrun anything on the water in that boat of his."

"You like him. I can hear it in your voice."

"Sully's a good man. Spent some time in Ireland as a gunrunner, he knows boats and how a criminal thinks because he was one a long time ago. No. Cyrus never caught him. You should get some sleep."

Her eyes were growing accustomed to the darkness, and she could see the outline of his face. Such a handsome face.

To be with him again seemed like a dream. Like the dream she'd had over and over again in the early years, after she'd fled Washington.

She had never been able to completely cut him out of her life. Deep down, buried beneath the layers of pain, her heart had held on to the memories. They were glorious memories. They had only been married five years, but they had lived those years so alive and so in love.

She shivered with the memory and he must have noticed.

"Need some more heat?"

He lay down beside her before she could answer, and this time she snuggled into him, angled her head up to look at him once more. She could feel his breath on her cheek and reached up and brushed her fingers over his lips. Remembered how much she had enjoyed kissing him. He must have remembered, too. His hand was suddenly in her hair and he lowered his head.

A single kiss that breathed life into the past.

A single kiss that had the power to rewind time.

Chapter 7

Johanna woke up cold and knew immediately she was no longer wrapped in Adolf's arms. She glanced around, searching for him, and found him standing at the mouth of the cave.

She sat up slowly and let her eyes drift over his naked profile. His bare back and broad shoulders. His amazing ass and solid thighs. His rock-hard chest and abdomen.

The ocean breeze lifted his silver hair and in that moment he looked like a Greek god. Johanna stared, her body responding to the sight of him, all of him. She was still naked from the waist up and she felt her nipples contract and turn hard. She wanted to blame it on the cool morning breeze rushing in from the sea, but she knew it wasn't the chill in the air. It was all Adolf and the memory of his lips last night.

Suddenly he turned his head and his eyes locked with hers. Like a doe caught in headlights, Johanna was unable to move, unable to take her eyes off him as he turned and walked toward her.

Stone perfection silhouetted against a pink sunrise.

"Morning." He reached for his shorts and jeans on the rock and pulled them on.

Johanna came out of her daze and brought her hand across her breasts. She knew it was foolish. He'd had plenty of time to look at her while she slept.

Had he? She knew his body wanted her, but did his heart?

She couldn't imagine him ever forgiving her for what she'd done. She hadn't trusted him enough, and that had sent her into another man's bed. His enemy's bed.

No, he would never forgive her for that. The truth was, she would never forgive herself.

She watched him pull on his boots. He wasn't overly talkative this morning. All business, so it seemed. Or maybe he was regretting kissing her.

"When do we leave?" she asked.

He looked up and the answer wasn't what she expected. "We don't."

"Why?"

He pointed to her leg. "The leg needs another day."

She glanced down at the bandage around her swollen thigh. "How do you know? I haven't even tried to stand yet."

He came to his feet. "I said we'll hold here another day." Then he left her in the cave, sitting with her hand still shielding her breasts.

There was no *maybe* about it, Johanna decided. He regretted the kissing.

Merrick did a search of the beach. It served two purposes. If Cyrus's yacht was close by, it would be easy to spot, and then there was Johanna... He'd spent the night holding her, and with the dawn he'd soaked up the sight of her half-naked, curled against him. He had to clear his had. Had to be at the top of his game, and right now, he was riding an emotional roller coaster.

There was no sign of any boats. Nothing but water. But he

was sure Cyrus's men were out in full force. As he headed back to the cave he scanned the rugged mountains. When he stepped into the cave Johanna was still naked from the waist up. He'd forgotten that her clothes were out of reach on a rock, and she again covered her breasts when she saw him. They were fuller than be remembered. He'd noticed that as she'd slept. It had reminded him that not everything about her was the same. She'd had a child. Cyrus's son.

"Where have you been?"

"I checked the beach. No sign of Cyrus."

"I think we should leave before he shows up."

"No."

"If you were alone you would already be gone from here."

"But I'm not alone."

With the dawn, he'd examined her leg, and, although they needed to get off the beach, she wasn't in any shape to go anywhere. He still didn't know what he was going to do about her bare feet.

He didn't like the situation, but there was nothing he could do about it. Cyrus would be out for blood. Burning the boat clearly was the action of a man who knew that Johanna had been on it—on it with his most hated enemy.

"Adolf?"

"What do you need? Hungry?"

She glanced at his bag. "Is there food in there?"

"A few freeze-dried meals."

"Yum."

The face she made pulled a smile from him. "Nothing but the best for my...for you."

He snagged her bra from the rock and knelt down behind her. "Come on. Let's get those pretty babies covered up." He brought his arms around her, looped his thumbs through the bra straps and positioned it in front of her.

She slipped her arms into the straps, then adjusted the cups around her breasts.

"One, two or three?"

"Two."

He hooked the bra in the second row of eyes. "Want your blouse?"

"Is it in one piece?"

The morning was already getting hot. The cave would give them some shelter from the heat, but not much. He said, "At the moment, but I could take the sleeves out of it quick enough if you want."

"I'll roll them."

He handed the blouse to her, then sat down beside the pack and opened it. They would need to ration the water. He set out the bottles he'd packed. Ripped open a package of nuts and dried fruit and handed it to her.

"Start with that."

She took the package, peered inside, then shook out a small handful and handed it back to him. "I never pictured you as a Boy Scout. Were you ever?"

"No. Just a wild street snot."

"You never told me much about your childhood."

"It wasn't too memorable. One parent."

"I remember that."

"She worked three jobs when I was a kid. I was left on my own a lot. Like I said, nothing memorable."

"Were we memorable?"

He was opening a package of dried scrambled eggs. He looked up. "Best five years of my life."

She glanced away, a glassy shimmer in her eyes. He made no comment, just got busy and poured water into the bag and resealed it. "Ten minutes," he said, "and breakfast is served."

He saw her touch the corner of her left eye, then her right. She cleared her throat. "What happens when we leave this place?"

"We find a village, take a shower, get some real food and some sleep. I'll get in touch with Sully, then Sly."

"Sly?"

"Sly McEwen. He's my second in command in Washington."

"Is he like you and Sully?"

"What do you mean?"

"A wild street snot with Boy Scout capabilities?"

"Pretty much. Over the years I've commanded a lot of men. But this last team…" Merrick smiled. "These men are…"

"Special?"

"Yeah. Onyxx usually assigns a commander to their chosen crew. A few years ago I convinced them to let me pick my own. After they agreed I went looking for six men. I didn't want normal military, born and bred. I was looking for something different."

"Men like you?"

"Maybe. Men who had seen hell and survived. Yeah, I guess, men like me. My superiors weren't crazy about the six I found. But before long the team had been dubbed the Rat Fighters. The most unbeatable team to serve Onyxx. They spent seven years in the trenches, and they've all survived."

"At your command?"

"Yes. Even though they were disbanded over a year ago, they all still work for Onyxx on some level. If I needed them they would be here tomorrow."

"And do you need them?"

"I was hoping I could handle this on my own. But maybe not. You said that Cyrus told you I thought you were involved in a conspiracy. Tell me more about that."

"He said that you believed I was a double agent and I was using the gallery to hand off secret documents about Onyxx activities to a Russian informant."

"The truth is, I did investigate Joseph Kravin, your boss at the gallery, for conspiracy. Because you were working for him, naturally you were investigated, too."

"Is that why you came to the gallery that day?"

"Yes."

"So our dates were nothing more than you doing your job?"

"Until the investigation was over, my job was to keep a close eye on Kravin and you."

"So it was business?"

"I'm an Onyxx agent, Johanna. Things are never black-and-white. Yes, it started out as business. When you showed up at Chadwick's three days in a row, you drew a red flag."

"So you pretended to be interested in me because you believed I was part of some conspiracy?"

"There was no conspiracy. After six weeks you both checked out and the investigation was closed, and Johanna Angela Banning was no longer of interest to Onyxx. But I couldn't forget you that easily."

"How did Cyrus find out about it?"

"Briggs. I told you he was Cyrus's mole at Onyxx. Peter had access to all of Onyxx's archives. Cyrus must have told Peter to find out anything that he could use to further his scheme to convince you to go away with him."

"And now Peter's dead."

"We suspected there was a mole in the Agency for a few years, but we couldn't find him. A month ago Cyrus hinted that it was Peter. Before we could verify any of it or get Peter to talk, Cyrus showed up in Washington and killed him. That's when he left me your ring and the note."

He opened the pouch of eggs, stuck the spoon inside and handed it to her. She took the bag, stirred the eggs and muttered something softly.

"What was that?"

She looked up. "I said, I liked your smile. That's why I gave you mine at Chadwick's. A smile, Adolf. A simple, honest smile. You were there that first day with some men. You looked so unapproachable sitting there smoking, the air above the table a cloud of gray haze. Big bad tough guys. That's what I thought. But then you glanced up and looked at me. And…"

"And what?"

"The smile you offered a second later… I'll never forget it. You were all edgy and very intimidating, but your smile was soft and genuine. That's why I went back the next day and the next, hoping to see you again. I thought the day you followed me back to the gallery it was because you were interested in me."

"I didn't want you to be anything but a beautiful woman, Johanna. Even under suspicion that's what I was thinking. Hoping. After the investigation proved that… Like I said, the five years we were together were the best of my life. Now eat your eggs before they get cold."

"You used cold water."

Merrick smiled. "You noticed."

She returned his smile. "Aren't you eating?"

"Save me two bites. I'm going to check the beach again."

When he got up and started out of the cave, she called to him. "Adolf?"

He turned. "Need something else?"

"I still like your smile."

Sly hadn't slept all night. When Merrick hadn't called by midnight, he'd tried to call him again. When that hadn't worked, he'd called Sully. When Sully hadn't picked up either, he knew something had happened and it wasn't good.

By six o'clock he'd called Ash Kelly and Pierce Fourtier. He saw them now as they entered the airport. Eva had insisted on coming with him, but he'd refused to bring her along. If something had gone to hell, he needed her safe in order to stay focused.

She was angry, but she knew he was right. She'd sent him off with a kiss and made him promise to call her as soon as he knew anything.

They were boarding the plane when his cell phone rang. He pulled it from his pocket and saw it was Sully.

"It's about time."

"Sly, I need you to…"

Sully's voice broke. "You need me to what? What's going on?"

"Cyrus got there first. He was there when I went to pick up Merrick on the *Aldora*."

"And?"

"I had to make a run for it to get out of there. He chased my ass for a couple of hours before I was able to ditch him. When I circled back…"

"Dammit, Sully. What happened to Merrick and Johanna?"

"No Johanna. But Merrick… I found a body on board the *Aldora*. It's been burned beyond recognition, but I think…"

"You think what?"

"I think it's Merrick."

It was afternoon, and the warm breeze off the sea had forced Johanna to roll up her sleeves. Her butt was sore from sitting, but every time she moved, Adolf would tell her to stay put and let her leg rest. That if the swelling didn't go down, they were going to spend another day in the cave.

He had moved ten feet away from her. He'd emptied his bag, and his gear was spread out in the sand. He was rechecking his supplies like a soldier preparing for a battle.

Guns, knives, medical kit, flashlight. A few things she didn't have names for. All those things told her that in the five years they had been married, he had purposely sheltered her from his dangerous job. That there were things she would probably never know about him.

But none of that would change the fact that she loved him. Had never stopped loving him.

"You should sleep," she said. "I'll stand watch."

The comment got a raised eyebrow and then he glanced at her leg.

"Okay, I'll *sit* watch. Just an hour or two. You can't keep going without sleep."

"Turning into a nagging wife."

"If that's what it takes."

He gave her one of those questioning looks. The one he used to give her when he was trying to decide how to handle her. She saw him rub his temple, and it brought her attention to the vivid scar.

"You never told me how you got that scar," she said.

"Brain tumor."

That wasn't what she'd expected to hear. "A tumor? It's a surgery scar?"

"A couple of years ago."

"But you're all right now?"

He looked over at her. "Don't I look all right?"

"You look tired. You need to sleep."

"I don't sleep when I'm being hunted. Bad move."

Using the rock next to her for leverage, Johanna pushed herself to her feet.

"What the hell are you doing?" He was up and striding toward her in an instant.

"I'm proving to you that I'll be ready to go in the morning."

"Sit down."

"Two hours. If you sleep for two hours I'll sit down."

He wrapped his arm around her waist. "You're going to fall on that pretty face of yours and bust your nose."

She shoved his arm away from her. "If you're not going to sleep until we get off this beach, then I need to get this leg in shape so we can leave at dawn."

"You're not ready to travel."

She hobbled a couple of feet. Held in the urge to groan pitifully. The pain was excruciating.

"One damn hour."

Johanna smiled through the pain. "It's better than nothing."

"You're a manipulator."

She eased back down to the ground. "How come a woman is a manipulator and a man has a stubborn streak?"

He grinned. "It's a man's world, honey."

"And he wouldn't be here if a woman didn't allow it. So you tell me who holds the keys to the kingdom."

He laughed. "Good argument. I've been put in my place."

"One hour," she pressed.

"One hour."

She watched him toss the supplies back into his bag, then stretch out and rest his head on the bag as a pillow. He left one gun out—a handgun that he kept in his hand. He glanced at his watch, then closed his eyes.

Johanna waited several minutes, then slowly pulled herself toward him a few inches at a time until she was sitting next to him. His breathing was relaxed, and she let her eyes drift over him.

She wanted to touch him, but she knew he would wake up. Maybe not. She touched his cheek, ran one finger along his unshaven jaw. Such a ruggedly handsome face, she thought.

She sent her fingers over his chest in a feather-light exploration. She ran her eyes down his long legs, settled her interest on his crotch.

"However you want me, I'm here," she whispered.

It was crazy remembering those words after all this time. But she wanted to remember now. All of it. Every memory that she had buried for twenty years.

He'd said that their life together had been the best five years of his life. She should have told him that they were hers, too.

He was living the dream. Merrick arched his hips, moaned and sank deeper into that sacred place where he'd lived for so long. The exotic scent of Johanna surrounded him and he reached out to stroke the warm, fleshy ghost beside him.

Her moist breath on his neck, then on his lips, he heard her say, *However you want me, I'm here.*

He spoke to her then as if she was real. "Hot for me. Take me there," he whispered, "take me back to the beginning. Take me back, my love. My wife. My life."

Stay focused.

Don't wake up.

Another kiss.

Another moan.

Merrick jerked awake to find Johanna leaning over him. "What did you say?"

"I didn't say anything. You were talking in your sleep."

"I don't talk in my sleep."

"If you say so."

"What did I say?" When she didn't answer, he sat up. "Did I give up a tactical secret? Planning on using it against me?"

"Go back to sleep."

He checked his watch. He'd slept forty minutes.

"It hasn't been an hour."

"Close enough."

He saw her lick her lips, and then he knew. "How do I kiss in my sleep?"

A blush surfaced on her checks. "I was just seeing if what happened last night was…"

"Was what?"

"Ah…as good as I remember."

"And what did you decide?"

"You were a little unresponsive."

"So maybe," he leaned forward, "I'll have to redeem myself." Merrick angled his head and kissed her. When he heard the little moan of surrender, he brought his hands up and cupped her face and, like a husband planting a seed with deep roots—deeper than a bed of roses—he kissed his wife the way he had in all his dreams.

When the kiss ended, she whispered, "You still love me."

Merrick ran his thumb slowly over her cheek. "I never stopped."

As the day slipped into evening Merrick noticed that Johanna had turned despondent. He thought back over the day, and realized that she'd started to withdraw shortly after his admission that he still loved her. He didn't crowd her, or badger her with questions, and yet he knew something heavy weighed on her mind.

When the sun set and the air turned chilly, he stretched out next to her again and gave her his heat. She snuggled warm against his chest and, without saying a word, fell asleep.

Holding her, he kept watch throughout the night. In the morning, sensing she was still in a withdrawn mood, he began to prepare breakfast again, wondering what demon she was wrestling with. He wanted to ask, but he didn't.

She would tell him when she was ready.

They shared more cold powdered eggs, dried fruit and water. He asked, "How's your leg?"

"It's not as swollen. I'm ready."

"Ready?"

"To travel."

He doubted she'd feel the same way once they started over the mountain, but he stood and started to pack up. He put the tac belt on around his waist with a slide holster, handgun and ammo. He strapped another gun to his ankle, then an MP-5 that hung across his bare chest.

He grabbed the much lighter tactical bag and slipped it on his shoulder. "The rocks are going to rip your feet to shreds. There's only one way to prevent that. If we're going today, you're riding."

"Riding?" She didn't move from where she sat watching him. "You can't carry all that and me, too."

He arched an eyebrow. "You don't get a vote on this. Come on, get up."

"I'm too heavy."

"You're light as a feather." He motioned for her to come to him.

She stood and walked slowly toward him, limping less than yesterday. He turned and squatted. "Wrap your arms around my neck."

"You aren't going to get a mile before you're exhausted."

"That sounds like a challenge. Is it the gray hair?"

"Don't be ridiculous."

"Climb on."

He heard her sigh, then she wrapped her arms around his neck. He stood, reached back and pulled her legs carefully around his waist and locked his arms around them.

"You set?"

"I'm here."

"Let me know when you need a rest."

"That's funny."

Smiling, Merrick headed for the mountain, his stride and pace matching his determination to get them away from the beach. They had been there too long.

Miles later he was still moving, the sweet scent of Johanna all around him driving him on.

Cyrus slit his captain's throat shortly after he'd lost the race with the *Korinna*. Sully Paxton had gotten away, and the moment it became a reality the captain knew what was coming.

With Kipler now at the helm Cyrus refocused on finding Callia and Merrick. For two days they moved up and down the Dodecanese, searching every island they came to. He'd put five assault boats in the water as well, all armed with six-man teams of his very best, but he hadn't heard from one of them.

He had retired to his stateroom, but everywhere he looked he was reminded of Callia. They had spent nights here in bed and, not having her there the last two had drafted a mental picture of her in Merrick's berth on the *Aldora*.

"Damn you, Merrick. I'm going to rip your heart out with my bare hands."

"Father?"

Cyrus turned to see Erik in the doorway. "I've sent the men ashore to search Halki. Do you want me to go with them?"

"No. Come in."

Erik stepped inside. "Can I do something for you?"

"No."

"Has Holic called?"

"No word from him or the other crews I sent out."

"We'll find her, Father."

"*Da,* we will find her." The burning question Cyrus held back was, who would they find? Callia or Johanna? He said, "Merrick will try to turn your mother against us, Erik. The longer she's with him, the greater the chance. You need to be prepared if that happens. I will bring your mother home, but she might not be happy about it. I'll need your help if that happens."

"You know you can count on me, but she wouldn't believe anything Merrick said. Mother loves us. There's nothing he could say or do that would change that."

Erik had no idea what he was talking about. But it didn't matter. They would continue the search, and they would prevail.

When his phone rang, Cyrus pulled it from his pocket. It was Holic. A glimmer of hope.

"What have you found?" he asked.

"They're on the island of Kárpathos."

"You have them?"

"No. I found where they camped in a cave near the shore. I'll call you back when we've run them down."

When Holic disconnected, Cyrus smiled at Erik. "Tell

Kipler to get the men back, then tell him to head for Kárpathos. Holic is on Merrick's ass, and it won't be long now."

Merrick spotted a shepherd's cottage early afternoon. It
was tucked in a narrow valley. He stopped, crouched down
and set Johanna on her feet. Then he stood and scanned the
perimeter, taking inventory. There was a donkey inside a
small wooden fence, sheep on a rolling green hillside, but no
sign of the shepherd or anyone else.

"What are we waiting for?"

Merrick glanced at Johanna. In the high altitude he had
noticed a change in her breathing. Her asthma didn't like it
up here, and he was concerned that any little thing might set
off another attack. They'd been lucky so far, but that luck
wasn't going to continue indefinitely.

"Adolf, come on. The place looks deserted."

"It's not deserted or that donkey and those sheep
wouldn't be here."

"Not everyone in Greece wants to kill us. Certainly not a
harmless shepherd."

He glanced at her and smiled. "I suppose not."

"I can walk," she said. "It's grassy here."

He took her hand and together they picked their way down
the hill to the cottage. Merrick was about to knock on the door
when it suddenly opened. He had his gun at his side, ready,
but it wouldn't be necessary—the shepherd who stood in the
doorway looked harmless. No, he looked uneasy. That made
sense. Out here in the middle of nowhere he probably hadn't
seen another human being in months. And Merrick's guns
were clearly visible.

He heard Johanna sigh in relief, glanced at her. That was his
second mistake. The first was not realizing that the shepherd's
uneasiness was well founded.

The force of a gun blast sent the shepherd out the door face
first into the dirt. Before Merrick could push Johanna out of the

way and raise his gun, a bone-crushing blow slammed into the back of his head and drove him to his knees. When he looked up, Holic Reznik was standing in the doorway aiming a Glock at his head.

"Right on time, Merrick."

From behind him, another hard blow took Merrick out of the game completely, and sent him sprawling in the dirt next to the dead shepherd.

Chapter 8

Johanna sat frozen in the wooden chair in the shepherd's cottage. She wasn't restrained. Neither Holic or the two men with him had touched her, except to insist she come inside. She'd been guided into the house past Adolf, where he lay stone still in the dirt.

She wanted to go to him, but that would have been a mistake. Holic's eyes were on her the entire time, watching her as the guards went back outside. Time lagged, and when the two men returned, Adolf was between them being dragged by his arms. They had beaten him badly. So badly that there was no place on his body that wasn't bruised or bloody.

Oh, God...

She almost came off the chair, but she caught herself. She looked away as he was dragged past her into a storage room. When the guards didn't come out immediately and she heard Adolf groan in pain, she said, "I don't want him dead."

"He's not dead…yet, Kyria Krizova. But it is only a matter of time."

Holic pulled his cell phone from his pocket. He was smiling, and she was aware of his soulless eyes going over every inch of her. She was reminded that too much of her legs were exposed, and they seemed to interest him the most. He couldn't take his eyes off her thighs.

He punched a button on his phone, then went back to staring at her as he put the phone to his ear. "I have recovered your wife, Cyrus. *Da,* Merrick, too. A shepherd's cottage in the hills two hours by foot from Kárpathos City. Your wife?" He paused to give her another long, appraising look. "In one piece. It looks like she has an injury to her leg, but as beautiful as ever."

Johanna held out her hand. "Let me speak to…my husband."

"She wishes to speak to you."

A moment later Holic handed her the phone. Johanna had no idea what she was going to say. She wanted to beg for Adolf's life, but that would be a mistake.

"Cyrus…"

"Callia, at last. Holic tells me you're injured."

"I'm fine. No, I'm… afraid," she said, suddenly realizing that fear was the only true ally she had.

"Explain to me how this happened, Callia? Why did you leave Corfu?"

She prayed that Zeta had left Greece by now with Sonya.

"Callia?"

"I was tricked. He was waiting in Naxos. I'll explain when I see you. When are you coming to…take me home?"

Silence.

"Cyrus?"

"What did Merrick tell you?"

She didn't dare let him know that she knew the truth. "What do you think he told me? More lies. Are you coming?"

"When have I ever abandoned you, Callia?"

"Never. I know I made a mistake leaving Corfu. Please don't be upset with me." Johanna broke down then. All the lies. Years of lies, and twisted truth. She had trusted him. Believed him.

"You're crying? You know I hate it when you cry."

Johanna cleared her throat. "How's Erik?"

"Anxious to see his mother. You have worried us both."

"I'm sorry. It's all my fault. I've been such a fool."

"The fault is mine. I should have ended this sooner. I will give Erik your love. You know you have mine. Is there anything else you want to tell me?"

Johanna stared at Holic. "Just that I want to come home, and…and, I love you."

"Let me speak to Holic."

She handed the phone back to Holic, her stomach in knots as Holic turned his back to her, his voice much quieter now.

Johanna strained to hear his one-sided conversation. She heard bits and pieces.

"Perhaps. He is resting uncomfortably at the moment. Should I kill him now? I think that is a mistake. All right. We will bring him along."

When he disconnected, Holic turned to Johanna. He was no longer smiling. "Cyrus will meet us in Kárpathos City." He stared at her bare feet. "How did you lose your shoes?"

Johanna scrambled for an answer. "He took them from me so I couldn't escape," she lied.

His eyes slowly rose up her legs to her bandaged thigh. "And the injury?"

"Sea urchin spines when he forced me to swim to the island after abandoning the *Aldora*."

He pulled a knife from his pocket, and that's when she noticed his crippled hands—both of them were missing fingers. Before Johanna could object, he sliced through the bandage to reveal the evidence of her explanation.

"I will clean the wound."

She wanted to protest. Didn't want him touching her, but that would have raised suspicion. When he bandaged her thigh again, he took his time, touching her far more than was necessary and in a way that made Johanna's skin crawl.

He was a parasite. A man who believed that all women were nothing more than toys to be played with. It was in his eyes, and in the way those eyes continued to examine every curve of her body.

When he stood, he motioned to one of his men to follow him and they left the cottage. When the door closed behind them, Johanna stood.

"You should rest, Kyria Krizova. It will be a long walk east to Kárpathos City," the remaining guard said.

"I want to see him," she said.

"Merrick?"

"Yes."

"Why?"

"To tell him his lies have gained him nothing but a death sentence. I want him to hear it from me."

"I believe he knows he is about to die."

"I want to see him on his knees."

The man smiled. "I don't think he can get to his knees. But if you wish to see him, I see no harm in that."

He opened the small storage-room door. Johanna saw Adolf on his side, his silver hair matted with blood. His chest was a mass of bruises, and his handsome face—oh, God… His eyes were swollen shut. A rope bound his hands behind his back. It had been pulled down and attached to his ankles. The pain had to be excruciating.

She kept her composure even though the sight of him beaten and battered made her want to cry and scream at the same time. She said to the guard, "My husband wants him alive. Loosen the ropes. If you break his back, you'll be carrying him to Kárpathos City."

The guard's expression clearly told Johanna that the idea of lugging Merrick back over the mountain held no appeal. He bent down to loosen the ropes and, as he did, Johanna spotted the shovel against the wall. She picked it up and smashed it down on the back of the guard's head.

The noise was sickening, the force snapping his neck.

"Adolf…"

"Johanna?"

"I think I killed him, Adolf. Oh, God."

Merrick fought through the pain paralyzing his body. "Where's Holic?"

"Outside with the other guard."

"Cut the rope," he muttered, wishing he could see her to make sure she was all right. When she didn't answer, he said, "The knife is in my boot. They missed it when they searched me. Cut the rope. Hurry."

He felt her hand on his leg, then she was searching for his Nightshade. "I have it." As she cut through the rope, she said, "Can you see?"

"Not a damn thing."

"Then how are we going to get out of here?"

"Does the guard have a gun?"

"Yes."

"Get it for me and help me sit up facing the door."

In a matter of seconds, Merrick was sitting with his back against the wall, the guard's gun in his hand.

"Keep the knife," he said. "Hide it in your clothes and go back out and close the door. Wait, are you sure the guard's dead?"

"He's not moving. Breathing. I'm not going to leave you here. You're bleeding and your face—"

"Do what I tell you. When Holic comes back, he'll wonder where the guard is. Tell him he's in here with me. Don't say too much. Make some excuse to go outside. Use your asthma. Stay outside. Don't come back in for any reason."

"I don't want to leave you. Please. I—"

"Listen to your husband, and this time have a little faith."

"This is not a good time to throw the past in my face, Adolf."

"Go." Merrick heard the door close. Heard voices minutes later. He leaned into the wall and pulled his legs up to steady his hand on one knee. Aimed the gun straight ahead.

He heard Johanna coughing. Heard her tell Holic the guard had gone in to check on *that lying snake,* that she needed fresh air. Hard to breathe. No inhaler. Lost it on the *Aldora.*

Holic told his man to go with her, then called out to the guard in the storage room.

Merrick steadied his hand on his knee. Heard footsteps. Holic called out again, then the door opened.

Merrick fired the guard's gun. He heard a curse, fired again. Heard a thud. Heard more footsteps coming fast. He couldn't see. Prayed Johanna had stayed outside as he'd told her to do.

"Son of a bitch!"

The heavy voice belonged to the second guard. Merrick fired a third time. Four. Five.

He kept the gun aimed at the door. Listened. Waited another long minute.

"Johanna!"

Nothing.

"Johanna!"

Still nothing.

Merrick shoved himself to his feet, the pain in his chest stabbing him like a hot poker. "Johanna!"

He moved to the door, his foot coming in contact with a body. A hand reached out and grabbed his leg. Then a gun blast echoed in the room and slammed Merrick backward into the wall.

Johanna was on her way back into the cottage when she heard the sixth shot. What she saw as she came through the door sent her into a panic. Holic and the guard were on the floor, the color red everywhere. Holic was struggling to sit up, one of his deformed hands pressed into his bleeding stomach, the other locked around his gun.

Oh, God…

She saw him raise the gun again and aim it at the wall. Her eyes followed and she saw Adolf slumped over.

"No! No!" She scrambled over the dead guard who had fallen backward out the door. Holic looked at her. "Bitch," he muttered, then he slumped back, and the gun fell from his hand.

Johanna rushed to Adolf and dropped down on her knees. She pulled him up, saw the blood oozing from his side. "Adolf! Adolf, say something!"

"Are you all right? I can't see you. Tell me you're all right."

"Yes. Put down the gun, I need to see how badly you've been hit."

He continued to hold it. "What about Holic?"

"Dead."

"The guard?"

"Dead."

He laid the gun on the floor. "You're sure you're all right?"

"Yes. But you're not. I don't know what to do."

His hand moved along his side, probing the wound. "Not too bad. Went through."

Her relief overwhelmed Johanna with tears. "I was so afraid for you."

"Find my bag and get the medical kit."

On her feet Johanna stepped over the bodies, searching the outer room for Adolf's bag. She spotted it and opened it, grabbed the medical kit. She heard a noise behind her and turned quickly.

Adolf was standing in the middle of the room with his hands stretched out. "Johanna?"

* * *

"You're right, Sly. That body isn't Merrick," Sully said. "I should have examined it more closely before I called you."

They were standing on the dock below Sully and Melita's villa on Amorgós. Sly could see that the ordeal had shaken up Sully. He said, "Burned bodies are hard to identify, but I'm sure it's not Merrick."

"When I saw that body…" Sully shook his head. "Damn. I didn't want it to be Merrick."

"None of us did," Pierce said.

"He's a helluva commander," Ash said. "So let's get out there and find him."

"Krizova could have him," Sully said. "He could have planted that body so we'd think Merrick was dead and we wouldn't come looking for him."

Sly was looking out over the water. He turned and faced Sully. "There could have been a shoot-out and Merrick shot Krizova's man before things went sour. But knowing Merrick, he wouldn't have taken down only one if he was fighting for his life." Sly looked back out to sea. "He's out there somewhere."

"You think he got away?" Pierce asked.

"Then, why hasn't he contacted us? It's been two damn days." Sully swore. "I should never have let him leave after he found out Johanna was alive. I've never seen him like that before."

Sly heard the frustration in Sully's voice. "This isn't your fault."

"I was too late, dammit!" Sully swore again. "By the time I got there the *Aldora* was on fire, and then I had to shake Cyrus off my ass. Maybe if I had—"

"You did the only thing you could do."

"I'm not used to tucking tail and running, Sly."

"I'm not either, but I've done it. We all have. You had Melita with you. You did the right thing. What purpose would it have served if you had gotten caught? Then you'd be dead, and Melita would be at Cyrus's mercy." Sly lit a cigarette and blew smoke. "I'm still wondering how Merrick found Johanna so fast. I thought you said he didn't have any leads."

"He didn't."

"Melita must have said something. Something Merrick chose not to mention to you." Sly sucked hard on his cigarette. "I hate this. Standing around with my thumb up my ass. You know I'm getting sick of this place. The tourists can have these islands."

"Maybe there's a clue on the *Aldora.*"

Sly's dark eyes locked with Sully's and he tossed his cigarette into the sea. "You think you can find her?"

"I'll find what's left of her."

"Then we dive and pray we find something."

It was late afternoon when Sully cut the engine on the cruiser and said, "It should be below us, unless the current carried her when she finally sunk."

Sly scanned their surroundings. He saw an island in the distance. "Where are we?"

"South of Rhodes."

"What's farther south?"

"Kárpathos." Sully pointed to a speck of land in the distance.

Sly thought a minute. "How far to that island, do you think?"

"Three miles."

"It would be a hard swim. The current is rough, but it's possible," Sully said.

Sly looked back down at the spot where the *Aldora* had sunk. "I'll suit up. Who's going to dive with me?"

"I am," Sully said. "I'm going."

After a long hour of diving, the search paid off. Once Sly and Sully found the remains of the *Aldora,* they surfaced.

Pierce pulled Sly into the boat, and Ash gave Sully a hand. Sly said, "She's partially intact. We need fresh tanks."

Twenty minutes later, they flipped over the side again, with Ash giving them a thumbs-up. An hour later, after taking apart the wreckage, they were back on deck.

Pierce asked, "What did you find?"

"Nothing. She's empty," Sly said.

"Now what?" Ash asked.

Sly turned his focus on the island of Kárpathos. "We head for that island."

"If Merrick and Johanna got away, Cyrus will be looking for them, too," Sully pointed out.

"Then we better find him first." Sly looked at Sully. "I know you want to come with us, but you need to stay with Melita. That was Merrick's order, and I expect you to follow it."

Merrick wasn't dealing well with the blackness that had suddenly become his world. Holic's boys had pounded the hell out of him. His face felt like a balloon ready to pop and his eyes were swollen shut. It would take days before that would change, and in the meantime he was no use to Johanna.

"Are you sure we're heading away from Kárpathos City?" he asked.

"I'm sure. The guard said it was east of here. We're going north."

Johanna had been leading the donkey at such a damn slow pace that there was no way they were going to find a village before dark. Hell, for him it was already dark.

"What time is it?"

"I don't know."

"Day or night?"

"Day, but the sun's going down."

He should have known that. He could feel the air changing.

"From what I remember of Kárpathos, the island is long and narrow, and there are a number of villages in the central interior. We should come across one of them as soon as we start down the other side of this mountain."

"Cyrus will be waiting for Holic in Kárpathos City. When he doesn't show, he'll know something went wrong."

"By then we'll be somewhere safe."

He knew she was trying to stay positive, but he could hear her wheezing. "So you've been here before? Kárpathos?"

"Yes. Diafani on the northeast coast."

"You were there with Cyrus?"

"Who else would I have been with, Adolf?"

He heard the irritation in her voice. She was still angry with him for cauterizing the wound on his side and making her help. He'd had no choice, and when he'd passed out, she'd thought he'd died a second time. He'd woke up to her screaming at him.

"I'm not riding this donkey much longer," he told her.

"You'll ride it as long as it takes me to find a village. Now shut up."

"How's the leg?"

"It hurts, but I imagine not as much as you're hurting."

"As I remember, you have a poor sense of direction. You can get lost in a shopping mall."

"Is that your way of telling me the blind are leading the blind?"

"Pretty much."

"You're alive and…that's all I care…about. We're headed north. If I…can keep these damn rags on my feet, and this don…key happy, we'll…run into a village."

She was struggling for air, and he knew she was on the verge of another asthma attack.

"Johanna, are you—"

"No, I'm not having another attack, but I need my…air to get us over…the…mountain. No more talking."

The irony of where they were had brought back an unwanted memory Johanna would just as soon forget.

She'd been to the island of Kárpathos briefly. Spent a

week here six weeks after she'd left Washington with Cyrus. It was here she had confessed to him she was pregnant, and the next day it was on the north end of the island that they had traveled to Olymbos from Diafani, where they had been married in the church Agios Konstantinos.

The sobering memory had put her in a dark mood. Cyrus had given her a new name that day. It was the day Johanna Merrick had truly died and Callia Krizova had been born.

Fighting her asthma and her sore leg with every step she took, she led the donkey another two hours through the dark. Johanna's mood suddenly lifted when she saw lights in the distance.

"Why are we stopping?"

"I see a village." Johanna opened the backpack she'd tied on the donkey and took out the tac belt. Adolf told her she would find a roll of money hidden in its lining.

"What are you doing?"

"I'll need money to pay for a room," she said. She found the money and stuffed it in her bra. Twenty minutes later she led the donkey to the edge of the village of Aperi. "I'm going to leave you here and find us someplace to stay."

"I don't like that."

"I don't care what you like, Adolf. Leading this donkey… into the village with a beaten man, with a gunshot wound is bound to get…us more than a few…stares."

He didn't argue, but that was because he knew she was right. He slid off the donkey, his hand remaining on the animal's neck. It was amazing he could even stand in the shape he was in.

Johanna reached for his hand and led him to a rock beneath a tree. "Sit down. There's a rock." When he was seated, she tried to pull her hand away, but he wouldn't let go. "I'll be back."

"Be careful," he said. "Cyrus could be here."

She pulled her hand free and gave him the leather lead for the donkey. "Not yet, and maybe not at all."

She pulled the rags off her feet, tied her blouse in a knot around her waist, then headed into the village.

Because of its location it was evident that Aperi wasn't a tourist attraction. It was quiet and steeped in old-age traditions, the whitewashed houses small with few amenities, by the look of them.

It also didn't have much in the way of accommodations, Johanna soon found out. She walked the village for over an hour before she found a room to rent.

The old woman's house was well kept and the two rooms she rented were clean. The reason the rooms had been left vacant was the price the woman was asking for the luxuries of running water and electricity.

The ground-level room had a stone courtyard and a private entrance. Johanna paid the woman for the room for four days. She was sure Adolf wouldn't agree to that. He would want to keep moving, but he was in bad shape whether he wanted to admit it or not. And she wanted to have the room in reserve, just in case.

Anxious to get back to him, Johanna slipped out the door into the courtyard, through a series of sheltered stone alcoves where tomatoes hung overhead and potted herbs smothered the air.

In the moonlight she saw Adolf sitting on the rock, his head turned to the side as if he were listening and waiting for her return.

Ten feet from him, she said, "It's me."

"Took you long enough."

"Worried?"

"Yes, dammit."

"Aperi isn't flush with rooms for rent. It took me a while to find one with more than a bed."

"What did you want?"

A place where they could hide out for more than a day, Johanna wanted to say, but she didn't. She knew Adolf's situation was driving him crazy. He couldn't see, and she had no idea how that felt. She could only imagine how hard it was for him. But he needed some serious bed rest.

She said, "Selfish of me, but I was hoping for a shower."

"Find one?"

"Yes. What are we going to do with the donkey?"

"Let him go. Before morning he'll have a home."

Johanna untied the bag from the donkey and hooked it on her shoulder. When she turned, Adolf was on his feet. She stared at his face in the moonlight. It was hard to look at him, to see what Cyrus's men had done to his handsome face. It would be handsome again, and his battered body would heal. That was her silent promise.

She realized in that moment that she would die for him. That's how much she loved him. In truth she knew he would die for her as well.

You love me.

I never stopped.

"Come on," she said, then she took his hand.

Merrick woke up in bed with an ice pack covering his face. He reached out and felt the cool sheet beside him. The bed was full size, but he was the only one in it.

"Johanna?"

"I'm here. Sitting outside in the courtyard. Doretta Basilio, the woman we're renting the room from, told me we're welcome to use it. I'll be right there."

He heard a chair scraping on stone. He pulled the ice pack from his face and listened for her footsteps.

"I changed the bandage on your side while you slept. Can you sit up?"

"Why?"

"Because I'm going to feed you."

"Like a damn baby?" He moved to shove himself up and realized that every muscle in his body was on strike. Dammit.

He'd never been this down-and-out in his life. He refused to groan out loud and tried to ignore the headache that was shooting daggers out the top of his head. He forced himself up against the headboard.

He felt something settle in his lap. "I didn't mean I was going to spoon-feed you. Without your eyes, I think you can still find your mouth. There's a sandwich on that plate and slices of apple. When you're finished go back to sleep."

He felt for the plate, picked up the sandwich. She sounded pissed. Probably because he'd allowed this whole damn thing to happen. He didn't blame her for being angry. He'd become a pain in the ass and no use to her at all. Which was a sour reminder that he'd failed her once again.

"I need to take a piss," he said around a bite of bread, meat and cheese.

"The room's small. The bathroom is smaller. It's on your left. I'll help you if you want, or you can find it yourself."

With sandwich and apples gone, the plate disappeared. She'd been standing close by and he hadn't even known it.

"Water is also on your left. On a small wooden table. It's only a foot and a half square. Don't knock over the lamp."

He found the water. Minutes later he found the bathroom. "I don't remember taking off my pants," he said.

She must have been standing in the doorway watching him. She said, too close to be anywhere else, "You didn't. After you passed out, I put you to bed."

Chapter 9

Cyrus squatted down over Holic Reznik's lifeless body. Two bullet wounds. A hole in his gut and one in his chest. Both wounds were deadly. Holic hadn't lived longer than two or three minutes.

"A dirt floor in a bone-bare shack muddied together with sheep dung. A humiliating death, but one you deserve for being a fool." Cyrus muttered, then glanced over to the other two men on the floor. One had been shot in a similar manner. Not exactly neat and tidy. The other man had a broken neck.

At first he thought that Sully Paxton had showed up and taken Holic and the men by surprise before they could leave for Kárpathos City with Callia and Merrick, but now he wasn't so sure that Paxton was responsible for Merrick's escape.

Cyrus stared at the cut ropes, then at the blood on the floor. It confirmed that Holic had beaten Merrick and tied him up. His gaze shifted to the wall and the bloodstain. The amount of blood was significant. A bullet wound perhaps.

He picked up the gun next to Holic's hand. After examining it, he stood and eyed the wall. He glanced back at Holic again, then the wall once more.

"You son of a bitch," he muttered. "You killed them sitting on your ass, and Holic got off one lousy shot. A poor shot or you'd still be sitting here."

That's when Cyrus knew he'd been wrong about everything. Merrick had help, but it hadn't come from a surprise attack outside. That help had been here all along.

He glanced down at the guard who hadn't been shot. He saw something shiny hanging around the man's neck. He bent down and grabbed the chain and jerked it off, and there, on the end of the chain, dangled Callia's wedding ring. The one he'd given her years ago.

Cyrus's face contorted, and he hauled back and kicked the dead man in the ribs hard enough to hear them snap.

He had no idea how the man had gotten the ring unless he'd taken it from Callia. Or had it been taken from her days ago? The guards would have searched Merrick before they had tied him up. He went through the guard's pockets and found a man's watch—Merrick's watch, no doubt—and a switchblade with the initials *A.M.* on it.

He pocketed the ring and switchblade, tossed the watch on the dead guard's chest. "There you are, thief. So you can keep time in hell." As he walked out of the shack, he yelled, "Kipler, torch the shack."

He slept for three days on his back like a corpse. Three nights, while Johanna watched over him with one of his guns within reach that she'd put in his bag with his gear when they had left the cottage. If anyone tried to hurt him again she would kill them.

The best place to keep a wary eye out for trouble during the daylight hours was from the courtyard. The room had one entrance, and the courtyard was it. She had noticed that when she'd rented the room.

She had claimed that she wanted a room with a shower, but what she had been searching for was the safest place she could find to give Adolf the care he needed to recover from his injuries.

The sunny days spent outside had baked her skin, but Johanna had continued her vigil. Her leg had healed, but her lungs still reminded her daily that the high altitude was her biggest enemy. She'd existed on the edge of panic that she would succumb to an asthma attack, and Adolf would wake up to find her comatose, or dead.

She couldn't let that happen, and so she tried to stave off her fears with something that would take her mind off her tenuous health. She hadn't picked up a pencil and sketch pad in years, but for the past three days she'd spent hours in the courtyard sketching. It was a piece of herself she had left behind in Washington—a piece of herself she'd lost along with everything else that Cyrus had stolen from her.

She'd left Adolf only once to buy food, clean clothes, sandals for her feet and a shawl for the cool nights. Afraid to leave him again, she'd sent money with Doretta to buy her sketch pad and pencils and to resupply the food. Doretta had been happy to do it, but Johanna had insisted on paying her.

Doretta had been curious about the man who never got out of bed. Johanna had made up a story that her husband had been beaten by thieves. Doretta had surprised her with an old remedy of crushed herbs made into an ointment—*to make your man heal faster, kyria.*

Each day she had bathed his body and applied the ointment to his cuts and bruises, and to Johanna's surprise his battered body was healing quickly. There was no more swelling on his face, and the bullet wound was no longer ugly and black, although every time she looked at it the smell of burning flesh came back to her. She would never forget laying that hot knife to his flesh to cauterize the wound and the agonizing groan he'd made before he'd passed out.

Seated at the table, the courtyard bathed in shadows, Johanna pulled her yellow shawl close and glanced through the open door. Before dark she'd gone in and turned the lamp on next to the bed. The dim light sent a golden glow over Adolf's face.

She left the courtyard, went inside and locked the door. Standing next to the bed, she leaned over and kissed his lips. Lips that were no longer swollen to twice their size. That morning she'd shaved him.

She pulled the sheet from his chest and kissed the fading bruises. Sliding her hand lower, past his hard belly, moving the sheet past his knees, she admired his body. In a moment of pure love and adoration for him, she touched his phallus, then pulled the sheet back up.

"You have no idea," she whispered, "how much I love you, Adolf."

She kissed his forehead, then went into the bathroom and took a shower. Minutes later, she climbed into bed next to him wearing only a pair of panties.

This would be the fourth night she'd slept next to him. Like the other nights, she kissed his lips and whispered a silent prayer that when he opened his eyes he would be able to see again. Then she slid her hand over his chest and turned off the lamp on the table.

Sometime in the night Johanna woke up to the sound of the shower running, a slice of light peeking out from underneath the bathroom door. She quickly sat up and tossed back the sheet. She was around the bed in an instant, the bathroom door swinging wide as she searched for Adolf. He was standing in the shower, the shower curtain open. The pulsating water was beating down on him. His back to her, his hands were braced against the stone wall and his head lowered.

"Adolf?"

He didn't move from his stance, just slowly turned his head. She realized she was holding her breath in anticipation, wanting to see his eyes. But they were still closed and her heart sank.

"Go back to bed, Johanna."

His voice was unfriendly. It didn't dissuade her. She stepped into the small shower and touched his arm.

"How many days, Johanna?"

She knew what he was asking. "Three days."

He swore, then shoved himself away from the wall and turned quickly, grabbing her by the arm before she realized his intent. In a blink of an eye she was boxed in between the shower wall and his naked body. She didn't think about how quickly she found herself there, or how he had known where she was to reach for her with such exactness. Not until he opened his eyes and she saw them focus on her face.

"Oh, God. You can see."

"You drugged me."

She had found the syringes in his medical kit, and there had been no hesitation to use them. Yes, she'd drugged him. How else was she going to keep him in bed?

"Yes," she said, "I drugged you."

"No sign of Cyrus?"

"No."

He ran his eyes over her face, then her naked breasts, past her flat stomach to her panties, wet now clinging to her hips and blatantly exposing through white satin the thatch of dark curls between her thighs. His gaze shifted to her thigh where she'd removed the bandage just yesterday from her brush with the sea urchin.

"Barely a scar," she said. "Can you see me clearly?"

His eyes moved back up to lock with hers. "Clearly. For drugging me," he said again. "What if you'd had an asthma attack while I was knocked out?"

"I didn't."

Seconds ticked by, then he cast his eyes over her again, and that look… She knew that look.

He reached past her and turned off the shower. "Tell me no, and we'll see if you can talk me out of it."

She didn't want to talk him out of it, but she didn't want this to be some contest either, and she was sure Cyrus wasn't far from Adolf's thoughts. She knew she was right when he spoke again.

"He take you in the shower? Everywhere we used to make love?"

"Adolf, please don't."

"Don't what? Talk? Take you? Think too much about who took you last?"

She turned her face away.

"What part of your body does he likes best, Johanna?" His hands found her hips, and his fingers caught the elastic of her panties. She thought he was going to shove them down, but he didn't. His fingers moved inside to palm her backside. "Is he an ass man? He squeeze you like this? Or maybe—"

"Don't." She tried to shove him away, but he wouldn't let go. He just kept moving his fingers over her.

"Did he take his time? Time enough to know what you like? To own you?"

"Not like this, Adolf. Not with him here between us. Please…"

He slid one hand out of her panties, and around the front, moved it over her mons and between her legs. She was already wet, anticipating what was coming. And he was coming, there was no doubt. His jaw was set, and his eyes were glazed with a fever that had nothing to do with his ordeal days ago.

And that look…it told her that he remembered everything that *she liked*. No man knew her better. Not even Cyrus. No man ever would.

She glanced down and saw that his shaft was stone hard, jutting up from between his legs. That there was a glistening drop of moisture on the tip, and that it wasn't from the shower. He wanted her as much as she wanted him.

His hands gripped her hips and he pushed her back against the wall. He was so close she could feel his breath on her face, the heat from his phallus as it touched her belly. She was losing herself in the moment. Losing herself in his eyes— eyes that could see her so *clearly*.

He bent his knees and lowered his head, captured one breast and teased her nipple into a stiff peak. Of her own volition Johanna arched her back. He was burning her alive with his mouth, and as she clung to the wall, he captured her other breast and gave it the same attention before he moved on, lower over her quivering belly—his tongue like a teasing dagger as it scalded her flesh.

He kept going until he was on his knees in front of her. His hands tightened around her thighs, then he brought his head up and looked at her. "Talk me out of it, Johanna. Last chance."

He knew she wouldn't. If he remembered everything else, he would remember that, once she was teetering on the edge, she was his and she would do anything, even beg him to take her. All this he knew as his hands moved up to the elastic on her panties and he slowly pulled them down. Not off completely, that's another thing he remembered, the slow tease that intensified his every touch. His every intent.

His hand went between her legs, and he hooked his thumb in the front of her panties dragging them down into a V, exposing her and parting her so slightly.

All her nerve endings localized there as he dragged his thumbnail slowly over her nubbin. A moan escaped her lips, and he played his wicked game over and over again, moving his thumb forward and back until she was trembling inside, and her hips arched forward in silent surrender to whatever it was he had planned next.

And he had a plan. He shoved her panties to her ankles, and then she felt the heat from his breath touch her.

Then he kissed her there.

Another moan, and then she was begging. "Adolf, please. Please don't stop."

He looked up again, his eyes disconnected. She realized then that Cyrus was still with them. She wanted to push him away as much as she wanted Adolf's mouth and tongue back on her flesh.

As if he'd read her mind, he slanted his head and covered her with his mouth, his tongue moving over her slit and sending her trembling and writhing against the wall like a worm caught on a hook.

She reached down and threaded her hands in his hair as he sent his tongue deeper, pulling another moan of pleasure from her, sending her headlong into an explosive climax. A climax that brought another lost piece of her old life back to her.

The old adage, possession is nine-tenths of the law, brought Merrick to his feet, and while Johanna was still in the thrall of nirvana, he pushed himself into her with one solid thrust.

Stone encased in velvet.

The feel of her sent him into a wild surrender of old memories. They fed his body, fed his soul, and suddenly all he wanted was to claim his wife.

Nothing else mattered.

He would make her his again. Dammit, he would.

He felt her body shudder, then give way to his single-minded invasion. He let out a harsh groan and lifted her up, seating himself to the hilt as she wrapped her arms and legs around him.

Face-to-face, he pressed her against the wall once more trying to control the pace. But there were too many years of pain and sorrow, too many threadbare emotions giving way to the hammering need inside him to take her.

Take his wife.

Her eyes never left his when she said, "However you want me, I'm here. Taking me in anger, or in love. I'm yours. I've always been yours."

Then she took his mouth, and made him believe it.

Life reborn.

In that instant Johanna came back to him.

No, Merrick thought, as the seeds of love for her separated from his body and passion claimed them both. His wife had never left him.

Chapter 10

"Closer," Johanna whispered. "I love the feel of you around me."

She melted against him and pressed her breasts into his warm chest. They were in bed all tangled up, legs wrapped in and around each other. He'd made love to her a second time after carrying her to the bed. This time there was no anger in him, only love.

A blissful love surrounded by tenderness. So much that it had shattered her, and she'd cried.

She was aware of the fragility of their reunion. Cyrus was still out there somewhere, and Erik...

Where was he? Was he all right? Would she ever see him again?

"You're quiet all of a sudden. What are you thinking?"

"I was thinking about Erik. Wondering if he was all right."

"I'll get him back to you."

She glanced up and the look he gave her was suddenly

solemn. She knew he blamed himself for everything that had happened. She'd blamed him in the beginning, but not anymore. Cyrus was to blame. He set this nightmare into motion and they had been forced to play his game. Both of them.

"Tell me about Washington."

"What about it?"

His arm was around her shoulder, and his fingers were playing with her hair. His free hand was holding hers, their fingers laced together.

"What's a normal day like for you?"

"I get up, go to work, go home, and…get up and go to work again."

"Do you still jog around the lake like we used to?"

"No. I moved out of the house not long after you…disappeared."

She frowned. "You sold the house?"

"No. I was going to. Listed it with a Realtor. Three times, in fact."

"And?"

"It's still ours."

Ours…

"But you don't live there?"

"I moved into the city and rented an apartment. But I moved back a few weeks ago."

"Why?"

He hesitated, then said, "Cyrus blew it up. My apartment. I was out of town on a mission. I got a call while I was away that the apartment building had caught on fire. Later, my investigation proved otherwise. It was C4."

"Did he know you were gone, or did he…"

"Want me dead? He's had plenty of opportunities to kill me. I'm beginning to think there's another reason why he's allowed me to live all these years."

"Allowed you? You make it sound like you have no choice in the matter."

"I've taken precautions, but there are plenty of ways to kill a man if you want him dead and you know where to find him. Unlike Cyrus, I'm not too hard to find." He looked down at her, then slowly kissed her. "Other than playing doctor, what did you do while I was dead to the world?"

"That's my secret."

"I don't like secrets. Tell me."

"I bathed you and…kissed you."

"You took advantage of a defenseless man?"

He was smiling now, and Johanna smiled back. "Guilty."

"That means I'm behind, and I should catch up."

"It would only be fair."

He pulled her even closer and kissed her again. Kissed her over and over again. Johanna lay there in his arms and savored each kiss. When the kisses began to move away from her lips, she closed her eyes. Then his hands were caressing her body, and his lips followed.

In the morning Johanna woke up to voices. She recognized both of them. It was Adolf speaking to Doretta. She sat up. The door was open, and Adolf was sitting at the table where she'd spent countless hours while he'd recovered from his injuries.

Roles reversed, she was now the one in bed. She couldn't take her eyes off him. He sat there in the clothes she'd bought him at the corner market. He'd rolled the sleeves up on the gray shirt, and he was wearing jeans. His feet were bare.

He had a five-o'clock shadow, and his silver hair caught the warm breeze. He must have felt her eyes on him because he slowly turned his head and their eyes met. He held her gaze a moment, turned and said something to Doretta, then stood.

Johanna saw Doretta walk away, and then Adolf was on his way back inside.

"Morning." He leaned down and casually kissed her. "Doretta brought by some kind of pastry for breakfast. You've made a friend."

She had pulled the sheet up to hide her breasts. She was naked and all too aware of why. Adolf had kissed every inch of her body throughout the night. Had made love to her again before dawn.

"The pastry is *loukoumades*. It's a dough fritter with honey syrup and sesame seeds."

"Doretta tells me there's a tour bus that comes through here on Saturday. I'm thinking we hitch a ride on it day after tomorrow. I need to make contact with Sully. He's probably wondering where the hell we are."

"If you think you're going to send me away, you can just—"

"I already tried that and it was a mistake."

Johanna reached out and played with the collar on his shirt. "Did you eat?"

"No. Doretta brought coffee, too. I've had a few cups. Want to join me for a bite of…fritter?"

"*Loukoumades.*"

"Yeah, that."

"I'll shower and get dressed, and be right out."

Without warning he scooped her up along with the sheet. Smiling, he said, "No reason to get dressed yet."

He carried her outside and eased her down on one of the chairs at the table. Seated next to her, he poured her a cup of coffee. "Fresh brewed," he said, setting it down in front of her. "It's good, but not yours. You always made the best."

He had always made her feel so important. She loved that about him. Loved everything about him.

Johanna reached for the coffee cup and spotted her sketch pad on the table. She knew she hadn't left it there last night. She'd brought it inside and laid it on the narrow vanity in the corner of the room.

He must have seen where her eyes had drifted. He reached for the pad and sat back and opened it up.

It was too late to snatch it away and hide the drawings, and she knew he'd already looked at every one anyway. She reached for the *loukoumades*, tore off a chunk it and took a bite.

"I see you're still drawing."

"Not really. That's the first since I left Washington."

He flipped from the first drawing to the second. "I thought your passion was scenery." He turned to the next drawing. Then the next. Still no scenery. He studied the drawing a long while, then glanced up, his sexy gray eyes smiling. "Dream man?"

She'd named the drawing he was looking at. She said, "You were the perfect still life." My fantasy, she thought, keeping that to herself. "While you slept it looked like you were somewhere far away in a dream."

He gave her a strange look, then went back to studying the drawing. "Good perspective."

"When did you become an art critic?"

"I'm far from that, but I've spent some time at the Fondo del Sol over the years."

"The art center? I used to have to beg you to go there with me."

"It was something you were interested in. A place you smiled a lot."

His admission set her heart pounding. He'd gone to a place where she liked to go to be close to her. "I'm sorry. I'm sorry for believing his lies."

He gave her a small smile. "I know you are." He sobered. "Cyrus does his homework. Over the years I've learned when he goes after something he doesn't give up until he gets it."

"Where does that leave us now?"

"I don't give up, either," he said, then he looked down at the drawing of the dream man, again.

She had boldly pulled the sheet away from Adolf and had drawn him naked from head to toe.

When he glanced up again, he said, "Dream man. What made you think of that?"

Johanna swallowed the bite of pastry. "I drew what I saw."

"You sure you weren't dreaming?"

He was smiling again, and she relaxed into a smile of her own. "It is what it is, Adolf. You're not exactly small…there."

"You would know better than anyone, I guess."

"Would I?" She had to know. "How many women have seen the dream man naked?"

He was taking a sip of coffee. He slid it onto the table, and when he didn't make an effort to answer the question, Johanna thought, *I knew it*. She hadn't believed him when he'd said there was no one in Washington waiting for him to come home. *Home*. Suddenly she wanted to go home. Home with Erik and Adolf. Back to Washington.

But what did Adolf want? She shouldn't feel angry or hurt that he'd been with someone. One. Probably several women. Who could resist him?

She hated feeling like a jealous wife, but she was his wife. She was the wife of *two* men, she silently reminded herself, ashamed now for asking him that question.

"The truth will be a little hard to swallow."

He closed the sketch pad and slid it on the table. "I haven't been with a woman since you left."

The look on his face told her he was telling the truth. And then there was the memory of how he'd made love to her in the bathroom. As if the dam had broken. It had broken again in bed twice more.

"I know. A man who enjoys sex as much as I do taking a hiatus doesn't make much sense, right?"

She made no comment.

"You going to say something?"

"I…believe you."

"That's it?"

What else did he want her to say. "Why?"

"I guess you kept getting in the way. I'm not saying I didn't take the necessary steps to survive. I just didn't use a partner. Not a live one anyway." He must have been waiting for her to say something again. When she didn't, he said, "I think that's enough on the subject." He took another sip of coffee.

Johanna stood and pulled the sheet closer around her. "You used to like to hold me in the garden on Sundays after breakfast. Hold me now."

He shook his head, but he was smiling.

"Shove your chair away from the table so I can have your lap. I think I'll still fit."

That comment sent his eyes over her curves. "Amazingly true."

He shoved his chair back, and she settled on his lap, curling her arm around his neck as he wrapped his around her waist. She unbuttoned his shirt and slipped her hand inside over his warm chest. "Do you know what I was thinking when I drew that picture?"

"No."

"You sleep very sexy. Like you're somewhere in a dream. Do you dream when you sleep?"

He hesitated. "Sometimes."

"What about?"

"You're going to think I'm certifiable."

"Not unless you really have been spending time with the dead. You did mention you don't have a living partner."

That made him laugh. The timbre of his voice, the sexy release took her breath, and she lowered her head and gently bit his earlobe, then whispered, "Tell me."

"You win."

"I always win when I'm in your lap." She wiggled her butt and teased his package, and as she knew he would, he answered with a solid response. "Now that I have your full attention," she said, "tell me what you dream about." She wiggled her butt on him again. "Tell me."

"Stop that, if you want me to focus on the answer."

She sat perfectly still, then wiggled once, and made him laugh again. Then his smile slid away.

"I started drinking heavily after…you were gone. A little medicine to help me forget, but I didn't forget. Guilt and booze is a bad combination. For me, anyway. I was pretty hard on the people who were trying to help me get through it. I started closing bars. Sometimes I made it home, and sometimes I didn't."

"What does that mean?"

"I woke up in parks and alleys a lot. Sometimes my pockets had been picked. One time someone had stolen my shoes. Anyway, after that I started drinking at home. Falling asleep wherever I passed out. One night I went to bed before I got drunk. That night you came to me in a dream." He cleared his throat. "I…worked that out on my own, pretended my hand was yours. After that it became a nightly ritual, going to bed before I got stink-ass drunk so I'd be sober enough for you when you came to me. I slept with your ghost, that's what I meant."

Johanna didn't know what to say. He'd kept her alive in his dreams. It was clear why he'd looked at her so strangely after she'd named the picture.

She leaned forward and kissed him, ran her hand over his chest inside his shirt. She moved her fingers slowly over his nipples, threaded her fingers through the light dusting of hair. She kissed his scarred temple, stroked his beautiful gray hair.

"I never imagined you would be gray this soon," she said. "When did it start?"

"I've been gray a long time."

"How long is a long time?"

Again he hesitated, then said, "Twenty years."

Her hands stilled. "Twenty? Twenty years ago your hair was coal-black. You don't just gray overnight. It's not—"

"The shrink called it traumatic stress. I was gray within a month of your supposed death."

Johanna didn't realize she was crying until he reached up

and brushed her tears away. "It's all right," he whispered, "it's all right."

"I'm sorry."

"Don't do that." He shook his head. "You have nothing to be sorry for."

She bent down and kissed his lips. Whispered, "Your wife wants to make love to her husband. Make love with me, dream man."

It was late afternoon and they had spent hours making love. He was sitting in bed, leaning against the wooden headboard, when Johanna came out of the bathroom. He'd been fully aware that her breathing was off again, and that she'd made an excuse to use the bathroom to catch her breath.

She had on her white panties and nothing else. Her long black hair pulled forward hid her breasts. She climbed back on the bed and sat looking at him.

"Feeling all right?" he asked.

"I'm fine."

"When did the asthma show up?"

"I had a lung infection. I couldn't treat it right away so—"

"Why not?" When she stalled, he said, "Equal time, Johanna. Talk to me."

"I was days away from delivering Erik, and I was afraid the medication would hurt him."

"So you refused treatment."

"Just until Erik was born. But the doctor said I had waited too long and that the infection damaged my lungs."

So Cyrus's son was the cause of Johanna's asthma. Merrick tried not to resent that. Resent the boy. He knew Johanna. How much she'd wanted a baby. She'd miscarried twice the year before she'd disappeared, and the fact that Cyrus had given her what she had wanted—what he hadn't—stung without a doubt.

"Adolf?"

"Tell me about your son."

"Why?"

He studied her and noticed a hot flush burn onto her cheeks. "Johanna, I'm not going to hold Cyrus against the kid. Not unless he's a chip off the old block. He's not, is he?"

She didn't answer right away. "He's tall and handsome. And very smart. He has my eyes."

Merrick saw that she was uncomfortable talking about this, but if he was going to go after her son, he needed to know what to expect. "How do you think the boy is going to handle it? That his old man is a nutcase and an international criminal?"

"I don't think he's going to handle it very well and, since I've been gone, I have no idea what Cyrus has told him about…us. At the shepherd's cottage I talked to Cyrus on the phone. I made him think I was still…"

"His."

"Yes. I remembered what you told me on the *Aldora* about Simon and Melita. That he'll use anyone to get what he wants. I was trying to protect Erik and buy some time for you in that storage room. When Cyrus finds Holic, he'll know I lied. If he tells Erik before I can explain, I don't know how he's going to react."

"He has to know the truth, Johanna."

She climbed out of bed, found his gray shirt and pulled it on. "I don't want to talk about this now."

"We're going to have to talk about it sometime. Now is the right time."

"Erik is in a rebellious stage right now. He doesn't always like to hear what he needs to hear."

"In other words, he's got his old man's attitude and bad temper. A chip off the old block."

She spun around. "He's strong-willed, but not bad tempered. There's nothing bad about him. He's…"

"He's what?"

"I've made some terrible mistakes. Too many." She turned away. "God, if I could just go back and do it all over again."

"Cyrus would have taken you that day whether you went willingly or not, Johanna. I'm to blame for that, not you. The kid's a minor problem, but—"

"A minor problem?"

"I meant—"

"I'm sorry you feel that my son is a problem. Okay, fine. I'll take care of my problem, and you take care of your precious mission. As you said, you didn't know I was alive when you returned to Greece. The mission is why you're here. How's that? You can take care of your priority, and I'll take care of mine."

Merrick stood and pulled on his jeans. "The problem is that, whether the kid understands or accepts the situation, he's going to have to deal with it." Adolf's voice softened. "If it'll help, I'll be with you when you tell the boy."

"His name is Erik. Stop referring to him like he's just an inconvenience. He's my son."

"Your son with Cyrus. I get it, Johanna. I'm fully aware of whose son he is."

Johanna hadn't meant to lose her temper or to hurt Adolf. And she had hurt him, she could see it in his eyes. She was so afraid. Afraid of losing Erik. Afraid of losing Adolf for a second time. It was too much, and the guilt… It was suffocating her.

"I just want my son and…you. Okay, I don't know if that's possible, and I'm afraid. Afraid of losing Erik's love. And… yours."

He wrapped his arms around her. "You'll never lose my love. You should know that by now. There's not one thing in this world that would making me stop loving you." He touched her cheek. "I'll find Erik, and when I do, together we'll— What's that?"

Holic's phone went off in Merrick's tech bag, and Johanna froze.

"Hear that?"

Johanna watched as Adolf turned away from her and listened as the phone rang again. She'd taken Holic's phone when they had left the shepherd's cottage. Adolf hadn't seen her stuff it inside the bag, but it wasn't because she'd been trying to hide it. He hadn't been able to see anything.

It kept ringing.

He glanced back at her, and Johanna was sure he saw the alarm on her face. He listened again, directed his eyes to his bag.

"I was going to tell you—"

"Tell me what?" He was already upending the bag, shaking out the supplies. The medical kit slid across the floor, a package of dried fruit, then Holic's phone bounced out, the ring filling the room like a damned dinner bell.

He glanced at her, then picked it up.

"It's Holic's phone," she explained. "I put it in the bag at the cottage."

The phone had rung three days ago. Johanna recognized the number. Knew it was Cyrus calling Holic to find out why they hadn't showed up in Kárpathos City. She'd thought it was a good sign. That Cyrus had no idea where Holic was. No idea that he was dead, and that meant he didn't know they had escaped to Aperi.

Shut up, she silently pleaded, praying the phone would stop ringing. It finally did, and then Adolf glanced at her again with an accusing look.

"He called a few days ago," she admitted. "Twice while you were sleeping. I never answered it. He doesn't know where we are. Stop looking at me like that. I didn't talk to him, and I was going to tell you about the phone!"

"The question is when."

To Johanna's horror, Adolf hit Redial.

* * *

Merrick glared at Johanna as he raised the phone to his ear.

"What are you doing?" she asked.

"I'm going to see what he wants. Or do you already know?"

"I told you I never answered the phone. I was going to tell—"

Merrick held up his hand, cutting her off as someone on the other end picked up. He waited, and then Cyrus's hard-hitting voice came over the line.

"I must commend you on your performance at the shepherd's cottage, Icis. It wasn't neat, but it was effective. Put my wife on the phone."

"Don't you mean *my* wife."

A demented laugh then. "It was a good trick. As they say, and timing is everything."

"I don't think Holic would agree. His timing was off, and well-deserved."

"You're starting to sound like me, Merrick. I always knew we had a lot in common. More than you ever knew, *da?* We share the same hate for each other, the same comrades, and the same wife. Brothers in arms. It is true, you know. I admit I'm addicted to the hate and our wife. How about you? You don't have to answer that. I know how much you hate me and how you've suffered. She wasn't with me a month before she gave herself to me. Did she tell you that? And, as you can see, I took good care of her in every way."

Merrick refused to be baited or show Cyrus any emotion or fuel to keep him running off at the mouth. Cyrus wasn't usually such a talker.

Johanna… She was the reason.

Melita was right. Cyrus was in love with her. *Addicted* was the word he'd used, but it was an addiction of the heart.

"So is she there? I'll bet she's standing close by, those beautiful eyes all questioning and serious. I'm right, aren't I? Put her on the phone."

That last was said with decreasing patience. Merrick said, "If you have something to tell *my* wife, I'll relay the message."

Silence.

Merrick was about to hang up when Cyrus said, "Did she tell you about our little secret?"

Merrick's eyes locked with Johanna's.

"I guess not. That can only mean one thing. She doesn't trust you. Tell Callia she can trust me to keep our secret safe. Tell her Erik is worried and asking questions. I'm wondering if I should tell him the truth or another lie."

"Her name is Johanna," Merrick corrected.

"Johanna is dead. I killed her. Even when Callia's with you, I'm with her. After all, we share a son and a secret. Tell her it would be wise for her not to wait too long to call me. Secrets are fragile things."

When Cyrus disconnected, Merrick closed the phone and tossed it on the bed. Then he swore viciously and said, "What's the secret, Johanna? The one you and Cyrus share, besides a son?"

The question came out of Adolf's mouth like a bullet, and Johanna staggered back several steps with vehement force. She tried to wrap her mind around what he was asking her. There was no secret between her and Cyrus. It was her secret and hers alone, and she hadn't shared it with anyone.

In that moment she knew a fear so palpable that the blood drained from her face.

Cyrus knew. If that was true, then he had known for a long time. From the beginning.

"No," she whispered.

"No, what, Johanna? What have you been hiding? What's the secret you've entrusted to Cyrus? The one he seems confident will make you pick up that phone and call him? A fragile secret."

"He said that?"

Johanna searched Adolf's eyes, looking for some speck of mercy, but there was only steely resolve and an unwavering demand to know *the secret*.

She'd waited too long to tell him, she realized that now. She was going to tell him, but she'd been looking for the right time. There was no right time. She should have told him on the *Aldora* that night, after she had learned about all of Cyrus's lies. But she was afraid then, and she was afraid now.

She couldn't stand the way he was looking at her. Accusing eyes. He had said nothing would make him stop loving her. If only that were true.

She turned her back to him to get away from those damning eyes, but in that moment he reached out and grabbed the back of his shirt, peeling it from her shoulders.

She spun around in her panties, her arm raised to shield her breasts. Half-naked, tears in her eyes, she shook her head. "I was going to tell you."

"Tell me what?"

"You don't understand."

"That's more than obvious."

He was standing there holding his shirt, his legs wide apart, his jeans low on his hips. She held out her hand for the shirt.

In answer to her silent plea, he tossed the shirt on the floor. "No more hiding, Johanna. I want the truth, and I want it now."

She glanced around the room, searching for her clothes. She spotted the shawl on the back of the chair. She headed toward it, but he blocked her path.

"I said now."

Tears shimmering on her cheek, her chin came up and Johanna dropped her arm to her side. "All right, Adolf. The truth. Here, with me stripped bare."

"I'm waiting."

"I told you on the *Aldora* that I wasn't sorry for how I chose to survive. I'll never be sorry because I wasn't surviving for myself. I was surviving for the child growing inside me. I was pregnant when I left Washington. Erik is yours, Adolf. The...boy," she emphasized the word, "is your son."

Her confession was punctuated with dead silence, and in those agonizing seconds his gray eyes turned to ice, then to arctic fury.

Her secret was out, and with it Adolf's love was gone forever. Then so was he. He scooped up his shirt and walked out.

Chapter 11

Merrick sat in the taverna a block away and stared at the whiskey bottle on the table. He'd ordered it thinking he was going to let that old, debilitating demon take him on a ride into hell—but he was already there.

I'll never be sorry because I wasn't surviving for myself. I was surviving for the child growing inside me. I was pregnant when I left Washington.

Erik was his son.

Her secret had shaken him to the core. Never had he once considered that the boy was his. He'd never asked his age, but the picture in her wallet was of a fresh-faced teenager—maybe fifteen.

He understood now why Johanna had been acting strange for weeks before Cyrus had abducted her. After her miscarriages the doctor had advised her to rethink getting pregnant. The chances of miscarrying again were high. She'd been devastated. She wanted a baby. His baby. She'd told him that countless times. He'd wanted one, too.

Merrick closed his eyes and considered all the pain she must have felt when she'd believed he had wanted her dead. The fear of how close she had come to dying with their child growing inside her. And how afraid she had to have been every day after that. Afraid she'd lose her baby.

I ran to save my life, she'd said. But what she had meant was that she had run to save the baby. Their baby.

She would have done anything to keep the baby alive. To keep him safe. She would have done it on instinct. A mother's instinct.

He had a son. A twenty-year-old son. An impressionable young man who worshipped the only father he knew, and Cyrus was that father.

The rage inside Merrick was steadily building. Cyrus had stolen his wife and his son.

Had he known Johanna was pregnant at the time? Of course he had. Which meant Cyrus had been spying on them in Washington for months before he'd made his move.

Perfect timing was Cyrus's MO, with the most collateral damage possible. He hadn't only wanted to take Johanna from him, he'd wanted the child growing inside her. The child of his most hated enemy.

For the next hour, Merrick tried to turn his rage into something more useful. A man on a rampage made mistakes. He couldn't afford to make any more. His wife had suffered enough, and Erik's life was in the hands of a madman.

Johanna had been afraid to tell him the truth, and he knew why. He'd reacted to her confession as she knew he would. Should she have told him sooner? Yes. But the truth was out now.

With the bottle of whiskey unopened, Merrick left the taverna. When he reached the courtyard he saw the door to the rented room standing open. He stepped inside, his gut instincts turning his renewed purpose to dust.

He saw his bag on the floor where he'd upended it, his supplies scattered. The phone was still on the bed. He stared at it, knowing she had used it.

Cyrus hadn't given her a choice and, by walking out on her, neither had he.

He saw the sketch pad on the table and next to it her wedding ring and a note.

I'm not sorry for the choice I made. Erik was all I had left of you.

Merrick pocketed the ring and the note. He bent down and starting throwing his supplies into the bag to go after her. That was when he noticed his 9 mm semiautomatic was missing.

Leaving her alone had been an asinine move. Merrick didn't waste time kicking his own ass. He would do that later. No matter how shocked and angry he was hearing her confession, he should have stayed. No matter what hard facts he had to face, he would do it for Johanna and for his son. He should have told her that.

He should have reminded her that, no matter what, he would always love her. It wasn't a choice. It was his destiny.

She had no more than an hour's head start on him, and after he'd put the fear of God into Doretta, she'd admitted her part in Johanna's plan to go to Kárpathos City. That her brother Anatoli had taken Johanna. That he was a vegetable peddler.

It was time to use the phone, Merrick decided. In the courtyard he called Sully, whose number was just one of many in his head.

It rang five times. "Paxton here, who's this?"

"Merrick."

"Where the hell are you? Hell, I thought you were dead, then—"

"Shut up and listen. Get Sly and as many of the men here as fast as you can, and—"

"They're here."

"In Greece?"

"Even Bjorn. Like I said, we thought Cyrus had killed you when he set fire to the *Aldora*. We found a body. Since we realized it wasn't you, Sly and the boys have been out searching for you and Johanna. Bjorn flew from the Azores and caught up with Sly."

"I don't know anything about a body. We had to abandon the *Aldora*. Cyrus showed up before you got there."

"Yeah, I know. I had to outrun him. So where are you?"

"On my way to Kárpathos City."

"I'll give Sly a call. Tell him to head that way."

"Good." Merrick hesitated, then came clean. "Johanna took off, and I'm looking for her."

"Why'd she do that?"

"I don't have time to go into it. Tell Sly to keep his phone handy. I'll call him soon."

"What do I do once I've called him?"

"Stay put. Cyrus is in the area. Stay close to Melita."

When Merrick hung up, he shouldered his bag and left the courtyard. Years ago he could do a six-minute mile. In good condition at fifty-two, he could do it in nine. He took off running, but on a bad road in the dark, with the sudden rain, the six mile trek would take much longer.

Doretta had told him her brother always stayed at a waterfront boardinghouse called the Zoltan. An hour and a half later, soaked to his skin, Merrick reached the city and, like a demon assassin on a head hunt with the clock ticking, it took him less than a half hour to find the Zoltan. He spotted Anatoli's vegetable cart still hooked up behind two donkeys. Without hesitation he entered the boardinghouse and asked for Anatoli Fedor.

When the woman hesitated, Merrick said, "I have news for him from his sister Doretta. *Kanete grigora.* Please hurry. It's important."

She motioned to the top of the stairs. Merrick took the steps two at a time, and without knocking swung the door open.

Anatoli was on the bed naked, a woman squirming beneath him. On the bedpost hung a bright yellow shawl. Johanna's shawl.

He flipped the safety off the gun on his belt and jerked it free and, in the blink of an eye, the barrel was aimed at the man's ass before he came to his senses and knew he had company.

"Get off her," Merrick growled.

The man froze, then he slowly rolled over. That was when Merrick saw the woman beneath him. Her black hair was short, her nose long and her sagging breasts red and feverish from Anatoli's unshaven jaw and admiration.

Undeterred, Merrick's voice still full of venom, he stepped forward and peeled the shawl off the bedpost and said, "Where's my wife? *Grigora!* Speak or die."

"Parakalo, filos."

"I'm not your friend. The woman you brought here from Aperi. Where is she?"

"At Pigadhia. The taverna up the street. That's where she wanted to go."

"Why do you have her shawl?"

"A gift. She insisted I take it to pay for the ride."

Merrick tossed the shawl on the bed, lowered his gun, then walked out. Johanna was meeting Cyrus at a taverna.

He left the Zoltan at a dead run.

The attack came in the alcove behind the Pigadhia. No one heard the cry for help. Too much revelry and merrymaking inside the rowdy taverna to hear a weak distress call. The street was all but deserted, the rain the driving force behind its emptiness.

Johanna was soaked and chilled to the bone, and still a sheen of sweat covered her face, the cords in her neck bulging.

She'd been fighting the signs of an asthma attack since she'd left Aperi on the back of a vegetable cart Doretta's brother had driven. He was long gone now, with a wave and a smile, clutching her yellow shawl.

The hard ground rose up to greet Johanna and she collapsed, the bronchospasm in full swing now. Her heart was racing and the wheezing was gone. She was minutes away from asphyxic disaster.

She dragged herself to a wall and pressed her back against it. Her situation was grave, and the outcome wouldn't be pretty. She knew what she must look like. Eyes wide, her face contorted, and the skin around her lips purple.

No oxygen.

Respiratory arrest.

Death.

So this is how it would end. She had dreamed of this. Woke up gasping for air.

Her tears were dissolved by raindrops as she floated on the fringe of unconsciousness. She saw him then, a mirage standing in the rain. Then the mirage came toward her and she knew she would live. He wouldn't let her die. No, never.

He had come for her. He had come as she knew he would. As he said he would.

She struggled against the blackness and pulled the gun from the pocket in her skirt. Too weak to raise it, the gun was knocked away easily, and then an inhaler was inserted into her mouth, with a command to breathe.

Johanna performed the ritual that would save her life, drawing on the inhaler. She sucked in the albuterol, holding the blackness at bay. But it would take her again. She was too far gone now, and the inhaler was no longer her lifeline.

A pair of strong arms lifted her off the ground. A harsh, barked-out order sent two men scrambling into the rain, and then Johanna was being carried off into the night as the rain came down harder.

Sweet tobacco mingled with his familiar masculine scent. His warm cheek grazed hers, and then he whispered, "I won't let you die, Callia. It's not in my plan. Not even God can take you from me. Not God, or Merrick."

Johanna was already gone by the time Merrick reached Pigadhia. Now for the second time that night he sat at a table. But this time he wasn't thinking about drowning his despair in the bottom of a bottle of whiskey.

He had searched the harbor looking for the *Starina,* but it was gone, too. No surprise there. Cyrus had gotten what he'd come for and again was on the move.

He was anxious to give chase, but that wouldn't happen until Sly showed up. He'd called him, and his agent had told him he was forty minutes away from Kárpathos City.

A pretty Greek whore danced by and gave Merrick a wink. He ignored her, checked the clock behind the bar. Ten minutes later he stood and headed back out into the rain. With any luck maybe Sly would be early.

The rain had slowed to a heavy mist, and he walked back to the harbor, searching for Sly's boat. He saw lights in the distance, heard the sound of twin engines at full throttle. When he reached the end of the pier, the cruiser approached but never docked. As it made a fast U-turn at the end of the pier, Merrick leapt on board and the *Marina* turned back out to sea as if she had a fire on her ass.

Sly McEwen and Pierce Fourtier stood at the railing. They were as wet as he was. Ash Kelly was in the cockpit piloting the cruiser, and next to him stood Bjorn Odell, his long blond hair tied back like a sea pirate.

Sully had told him they had found a body on the *Aldora.* That they had believed it was him. He said to Sly, "You identify the body on the *Aldora?*"

"No, but I think it was one of Cyrus's men."

Pierce said, "No sign of Cyrus on our way in."

"I didn't expect you'd run into him. He's headed for one of his hideouts by now."

"You look like hell. Fill us in," Sly said. "You didn't say much on the phone."

"Tell Ash to drop anchor. I'll give you twenty minutes."

Below deck, gathered in the galley with his men, Merrick sat at the table and summarized the past week and a half. He explained how he'd found Sonya Poulos, and muscled Zeta into bringing Johanna to him in Hora on the island of Naxos.

He told them about abandoning the *Aldora* because of engine trouble. Confessed Johanna had sabotaged it, and why. How they'd ended up on a beach on Kárpathos. How the sea urchin spines in Johanna's leg had forced them to hide out in a cave for two days before traveling into the interior. Their run-in with Holic Reznik. That he was dead, shot by a blind man with his back against the wall.

"Holic's dead." Bjorn was leaning against the counter sipping on a bottle of beer. "You're sure he's dead?"

"I'm sure."

"Your eyes were swollen shut when you shot Holic. How do you know you killed him? That bastard's got nine lives."

Bjorn and Holic's rivalry went way back. He'd been a thorn in his agent's side for years. Long before Bjorn had married Nadja Stefn. Holic's wife Mady was Nadja's sister. And Holic and Mady's daughter Prisca was now hidden away in the Montana mountains, sharing her life with Jacy Madox.

"I guess he was on life number nine then," Merrick said. "The storage room was small. I couldn't miss. I aimed and fired twice. Holic went down. I got up and he fired once. A wild shot that caught me above my hip."

"But he was dead when you left the cottage?" Bjorn asked. "You're sure?"

"He's dead."

Bjorn grinned, raised the beer bottle and said, "To blind aim."

"What happened after that?" Ash asked.

"Johanna and I headed for the closest village we could

find. Johanna was my eyes," Merrick admitted. "She took us over the mountain to the village of Aperi. I was in bad shape, and she was exhausted. She has asthma. We got a room and waited until I could see again."

Ash asked, "Why didn't you use Holic's phone days ago and check in?"

"I didn't know Johanna had picked it up when we left the shepherd's cottage. I admit that I never thought about it when we left. I just wanted to get her out of there. I realized she took the phone when Cyrus called today."

"Was he calling Holic?"

"No. He'd been to the cottage. He knew Holic was dead."

"So why was he calling?"

"He called to speak to Callia."

"Callia?" Pierce shook his head. "You mean Johanna?"

"She's Johanna to me, and Callia to Cyrus. When he married her he gave her a different name. Melita told me that Cyrus is in love with Callia. I think she's right."

"Or maybe he just wants what is yours," Sly said.

"I thought that at first, but he sounded anxious on the phone. In all the years he's been raising hell, the one thing that was constant was his self-control. Today, he seemed desperate. I think in the beginning he took Johanna out of pure revenge, but over the years that's changed." Merrick glanced at each one of his men. Then he said, "I have a son."

Bjorn's beer bottle never made it to his lips. "A son?"

Pierce said, "Are you sure, or is this just another one of Cyrus's twisted games?"

"You can't trust anything Cyrus says," Ash reminded.

"It's true. Johanna was pregnant when she left Washington. She confirmed it. The boy Cyrus has been raising is mine."

"Then he's no boy," Sly said. He's—"

"Twenty," Merrick supplied. "When Cyrus called he implied he and Johanna had a secret. When I got off the phone I asked her what it was. No, I *demanded* that she tell me. I didn't handle the news too well. I took off, and when I got back to the room she was gone. She left the phone and a few other things. She must have called Cyrus."

"He used the boy to get her back," Bjorn said.

"I'm sure he did. That's when I called Sully, then I took off, hoping I could stop her. I found the guy who brought her to Kárpathos City. He said he dropped her off at the Pigadhia. I called you when I got to the bar and knew I was too late."

"So where do we go from here?" Pierce asked.

Merrick stood, his exhaustion evident, but there was no time for sleep. He said, "Get this cruiser back on the water." He locked eyes with Sly. "Sully said you two found the *Aldora*. Can you find her again?"

"I can."

"How intact was she went she went down?"

"Shell's there, inner framework."

"Galley?"

"Mostly intact. Why?"

"My phone is in the cupboard. I stashed it in a dead-letter box. I didn't have time to get it when we had to abandon the cruiser."

Sly said, "It's not the phone that interests you, is it? What's in that waterproof container?"

"My GPS. Before I knew Johanna was tricked into leaving Washington, I thought she'd left with Cyrus willingly. I don't feel good about thinking that, but when I found her I planned to use her to draw Cyrus out in the open. Just him and me. Johanna was wearing his ring. I took it from her and placed a tracker under the diamond."

"And Johanna has the ring?"

"No. It was in my pocket. One of Holic's men took it from me at the cottage when he searched me. I saw him put it on a chain around his neck."

"Then it could still be at the cottage," Sly said.

Pride and ego, Merrick thought. When he'd seen

Johanna's ring on the table at the room in Aperi, he had instinctively put it in his pocket. Yeah, pride and ego were a man's weakness. He had plenty, but Cyrus had more.

He said, "When I learned the truth from Johanna that Cyrus had tricked her, my plans changed."

"You think Cyrus took the ring off Holic's man at the shepherd's cottage?"

"I know it's a long shot, but we don't have anything better at the moment. Cyrus is a detail man. He never lets anything go unchecked. If he found the ring, it's back on Johanna's finger, and the GPS will lead me to her."

Bjorn smacked Ash in the chest. "Come on. Let's get this cruiser dancin'. We got booty to find."

Johanna woke up with an invisible brick pressing down on her chest. She turned her head slowly from side to side and knew she was on the *Starina*. She recognized the stateroom.

She had shared this bed with Cyrus many times. The thought of being in it again sickened her, and if she hadn't been so weak she would have climbed out and set it on fire.

She could hear his voice. Cyrus was on the other side of the door and he was yelling at someone who was promising that his wife would live.

Cyrus was threatening the man's life. "Damn right my wife will live, or you won't."

She realized then that her arm was strapped down. She must have crashed. She knew the drill. She'd been there a few times before. The intravenous theophylline flowing through her vein was slowly stabilizing her. There was also an epinephrine injection on the nightstand.

She'd been close to death, and that explained why she was feeling so lethargic and exhausted. It took all her strength to shove herself up against the headboard and see she was wearing a white satin robe.

The lights were dimmed and they cast a golden hue over

the luxury suite. It was all so familiar, the sweeping white-leather sofa lined with ocean-blue pillows, the mirror above the bed. A statue of Zeus holding a lightning rod at the entrance to the bathroom.

The door opened and Cyrus stepped inside. He closed the door and, to her surprise, when he saw her sitting up, he smiled. She didn't return it.

"You're awake. I was beginning to wonder if that damn doctor knew what he was doing."

"It appears so. I'm alive."

"You've been as still as death for hours."

"He saved my life."

"No. I saved it, Callia." He pointed to Zeus. "And the earth shook with the proclamation that…she is mine."

He sat down next to her on the bed, and she recoiled at the thought of him touching her.

"You don't have to be afraid of me. I would never hurt you."

"But you did," she said. "Twenty years ago. You ripped my heart out."

"But I gave you a new one to replace it."

No remorse, not even a hint of regret on his face. His face. She suddenly remembered Adolf telling her that Cyrus had changed his face. That he'd had plastic surgery. Such a familiar face, but it wasn't his. He had told her so many lies. The frightening thing was that she knew she would have gone on forever at his side, believing everything that came out of his mouth, if Adolf hadn't opened her eyes. Hadn't found her.

"Where's Erik?"

"On deck, anxious for you to wake up."

"I'm awake. I want to see him."

"And our son wants to see you, too. He's been very worried."

"Merrick's son."

"That's just biology."

She had to know. "Why?"

"Why did I take you from Merrick and become Erik's father?"

"Yes."

"Because Merrick didn't deserve you. He left me for dead. Did he tell you?"

"Yes. In Prague."

"He left me in a minefield, still alive with no face."

"He believed you were mortally wounded."

"Then he should have put me out of my misery. I crawled out of that minefield on my belly. I ate rats and dirt to survive. I cursed him every day. But you know the old saying. 'What doesn't kill you makes you stronger.' You can relate to that. You believed you were going to die in that warehouse in Washington. Given the situation, you grabbed the first lifeline you saw."

"And you made sure that was you."

"Cyrus to the rescue. Right on time."

"You knew I was pregnant."

He brushed a strand of black hair away from her shoulder, and Johanna shrugged away from his touch.

"*Da,* I knew. I knew the day you found out. I was at the clinic. You left crying. You were pregnant. Something you desperately wanted. But the odds weren't good. Less than a fifty-percent chance you could carry the baby past the first trimester. Yes, I know it all. I read your medical file. You'd been down that road before, and it had ended badly."

Johanna looked away, unable to wipe away the pain of losing her unborn children.

"It was that bad news that made you decide not to tell Merrick about the pregnancy. I knew you wouldn't. It was fragile news. You'd been disappointed before, and you'd disappointed him, too."

"You're a monster."

"You didn't think so at the time. In fact, you were very eager to share my bed, as I remember. I knew you would do that, too. You would need to pass your child off as mine to keep it safe. After all, you had nowhere to go, and the only one willing to help you was me. You sold your body and Merrick's child to me in return for your safety."

"You planned that, too?"

"I planned it all, Callia. Two years of master-planning to take everything from Merrick, and it all started with you."

"You knew what I would do before I knew myself."

"No money. No home. A fragile pregnancy. Betrayed by her husband. A fugitive on the run. I expected no less from you. In fact, I would have been disappointed if you hadn't come to me that night. You didn't have much time. You were already four weeks pregnant. And as luck would have it, Erik was born two weeks overdue. Your secret was safe, or so you thought."

"All the lies," Johanna muttered. "Twenty years of lies."

"Not everything was a lie. In the spy world it's called the kiss of death when you begin to care about your captive. As you know, I don't like weakness in others, or myself. But you are mine. I was unprepared for that, or how easy it was to become your husband in every sense of the word."

"If you care about me, then do the right thing. Let us go."

"Back to Merrick? I think you've misunderstood my reason for confessing my weakness, Callia. I've come to realize that my weakness is my strength. That without you as the prize, my revenge on Merrick means nothing. I would have preferred that you never learn the truth, but now that you have, we must go on from here and rebuild what we once had."

Johanna felt a tear roll down her cheek.

"None of that, now." He reached up and wiped the tear away. "You know I don't like to see you cry."

"Are you taking us back to Corfu?"

"It would be foolish to return to Corfu, and from what I've told you, you know I'm not a fool."

"Then where?"

He didn't answer. Instead he pulled something from his pocket and opened his hand. "I believe this is yours. Give me your hand."

Johanna stared at the wedding ring. His ring. The one Adolf had taken from her when they were in the cab in Naxos.

"Where did you get that?"

"I found it at the shepherd's cottage. One of Holic's men had it on a chain around his neck." He took her hand and slipped the ring onto her finger. "Did you leave Holic's phone for Merrick as I instructed?"

"Yes."

"Good. I'll let him sweat a few days, then give him a call. I'm sure he's anxious to meet Erik." He leaned forward and kissed her forehead, then stared at her. "In a few days we'll consummate our new alliance. I would take you now, but you're much too fragile for what I have in mind."

He stood and towered over her, pointed to the inhaler on the nightstand. "You shouldn't need that, but it's there in case you do. I'll tell Erik you're awake." He motioned to an air vent high on the wall. "I can see and hear everything. Don't be foolish. If Erik should learn that I'm not his father, I would have no reason to keep him alive, would I, Callia?"

"My name is Johanna."

"As I told Merrick, Johanna is dead. And remember, it's Callia I want in my bed when I reclaim your body, so don't forget what I like."

"I won't come to you willingly. You must know that now."

"You will…*come*, Callia. Erik hates Merrick. I've seen to that. I can make him hate you, too. Or you can think of it another way. Everything you've done, you've done for your son's safety. And everything you will do from this day on will determine his future health.

"Rest now. Erik will be down to see you soon."

* * *

Johanna cried herself to sleep. She didn't hear the door open or the bed move under the weight of his body. It was the familiar touch on her cheek that brought her awake.

She opened her eyes and there was Erik, staring at her, his face drawn with concern. She didn't want him to worry. Didn't want anything to ever hurt him.

He had his father's stubborn jaw, and when he smiled, it was Adolf's smile. Over the past year he'd changed so much. Those heavy black eyebrows and that masculine mouth. The slight wave of his black hair as it moved over his forehead and the nape of his neck. The edgy way he carried his body with confidence.

It was all Adolf, even though he had her hazel eyes and her nose. And her weakness for art. He was a beautiful artist. That's why she'd wanted him to go to college.

She reached up and brushed a stubborn strand of hair out of his eyes. "What's this, no smile for me?" she said, trying to lift the worry from his handsome face.

"You look better. You really scared me."

"I'm sorry."

"You're back now, and the medication will work again. It always does."

"Yes, it does. You know how it is. A little sluggish today. Sleepy tomorrow. But I'll be up moving around before you know it." She forced a smile. "I'll be nagging you about something you don't want to hear before long."

That made him grin, and she drank in his beautiful smile. She loved him so much. Had been so afraid during her entire pregnancy that she would lose him. Lose the only part of Adolf she had left. Afraid now that she might still lose him.

He stood and walked to the port window. He wore jeans and a black T-shirt. He was all muscle and no longer a boy. The young man before her was strong in appearance and in his conviction.

"Father was right."

Johanna frowned. "Right about what?"

"He said he'd get you back." He turned around. "You shouldn't have left Corfu."

Yes, she should have, but she couldn't explain why. She wanted to. Wanted her old life back and wanted Erik to know his father. But she knew that wasn't possible right now. She could have stayed with Adolf, knowing she would be safe with him, but she couldn't abandon Erik.

"I suppose not," she said, remembering the air vent.

"I know the truth, Mother."

"What truth, Erik?"

"Father told me about Merrick. I've known about him for a long time. They used to work together years ago for a government agency called Onyxx, before Merrick became a traitor. He's been hunting father for years."

So Cyrus had twisted the story around completely and sold it to Erik. She wasn't surprised. Suddenly she remembered something that Adolf had told her that first night on the *Aldora*. Simon was dead, and he'd died because Cyrus had involved him in his vendetta against Onyxx and Adolf. The next thing out of her son's mouth confirmed her worst fear.

"Father is going to kill Merrick, and I can't wait."

Johanna's heart began to race as she studied her son. It was all there in front of her, and she hadn't seen it before now. Erik had changed in the past year. His newly muscled-up body, the hostile attitude. Cyrus had a plan for Erik, too, and it wasn't college. He was training Erik to become him.

She glanced at the air vent, knew that Cyrus was watching them from somewhere on the yacht, that he was listening to every word Erik said. Listening and watching her reaction.

If Erik should learn that I'm not his father, I would have no reason to keep him alive...

"This isn't your fight, Erik. Your father—"

"How can you say that? Merrick is my enemy as much as he is Father's. You don't have to shelter me any longer, Mom. I'm old enough to handle the truth and to stand beside Father when he faces Merrick."

"No!"

"Yes! Merrick is going to die, and I'm going to be there when he does. If I'm lucky, it'll be my bullet that kills him."

"Stop it!" Johanna gasped, her lungs not able to keep up with her word volley any longer. "Erik…please."

Talking to him was useless. There was no way she was going to make Erik understand. She couldn't say enough. Couldn't tell him the truth. She wasn't even sure that if she did it would make a difference. Cyrus had fed Erik too many lies and it had filled him up with hate.

At that moment she realized that Erik was more Cyrus's son than hers, and that Cyrus had planned that, too.

He'd stolen her life, and her son.

Erik hates Merrick. I've seen to that. I can make him hate you, too.

Chapter 12

Cyrus stood on deck of the *Starina* as the yacht sailed out of the Dodecanese, bypassing the Cyclades and headed for the Ionian Sea.

By tomorrow they would reach the island of Paxi. He had Callia back and his thoughts turned to Melita. One more detail to attend to and then he would finally end the game.

He was ready. He hadn't realized just how ready until he'd seen Erik's performance with Callia moments ago. From the monitor in the next room he'd listened to the exchange. Watched the scene unfold.

Callia was at his side again, and Melita would be soon. Then the only thing left to do would be to send Merrick to hell where he belonged.

A grave for two, he thought, his eyes shifting to Erik, who stood looking out to sea. He noted his stance, the way the wind caught his hair—Merrick's hair. At a distance he was Merrick in his younger years. An irritating fact he'd had to swallow year by year as the boy had lost his gangly youth and headed into manhood.

Over the past year he'd grown more anxious each day. He prided himself on his patience, had lived years biding his time until Erik grew up. But the last few years he'd seen the changes. The boy had steadily grown into the man he despised.

Even the boy's mannerisms had developed into Merrick's. It had taken every ounce of his patience to be in the same room with him. But very soon he wouldn't have to look at Merrick's son any longer.

Callia would mourn his death, but that would be her punishment for her betrayal, and she had betrayed him with Merrick. He had seen it in her eyes.

Yes, he loved her—that was his weakness—but he would never forgive her for being unable to give him the son he'd asked for. Oh, she had tried, with another miscarriage to her credit. That was the only part of his plan he hadn't been able to accomplish. But it wasn't his failure, it was hers. If she hadn't failed, she would have a son to replace the one he was about to take from her.

"Erik," Cyrus motioned for him, and watched as Merrick's seed walked across the deck, his natural swagger so familiar. "Find Kipler and tell him I want double guards on deck tonight."

Erik glanced back out to sea. "Merrick couldn't catch up to us this fast, Father."

"Don't underestimate Icis, Erik. He's the deadliest agent that was ever recruited at Onyxx. He managed to kill three men in that shepherd's shack after being beaten to a bloody pulp."

"When you talk about him it's almost as if…"

"As if what?"

"You admire him."

"I admire talent and skill. Merrick has both. He's a mastermind when it comes to the hunt and the perfect kill. I learned a lot of what I know from him."

"I'll tell Kipler." He started to walk away.

"Erik."

He turned back. "Yes, Father?"

"Good job today." Cyrus followed up his praise with a liquid smile potent enough to charm a snake.

When the boy scurried off to do his bidding, Cyrus headed back down the companionway. He met the doctor his men had shanghaied from Kárpathos City to attend to Callia, and the minute he saw the man's grim face he knew something was wrong.

"What is it?" he demanded.

The doctor was nervous as he backed down the stairs. "*Parakalo*, Kirie Krizova. She was doing fine, but now... I don't understand it. Perhaps a slight overdose of—"

"Overdose!" Cyrus grabbed the hundred-pound doctor by the throat and threw him down the last six steps as he charged down the stairs and threw open the stateroom door.

The smell of vomit reached him, and his eyes fastened on his wife. Callia was making that wheezing noise he hated. The one that warned him that her lungs were regressing. That there was a real possibility the damn doctor had given her the wrong drug.

He spun around and, as the scrawny doctor came through the door, Cyrus's long reach snagged him by the hair and dragging him farther into the room. "Fix her, or you will be quartered and tossed overboard as fish bait, you son of a bitch!"

"*Amésos*," he promised. "Right away. But she is very sick."

"Then you know where you're going to be all night, don't you?" Cyrus sat down beside his wife and brushed her hair away from her cheek. "Callia, can you hear me?"

She opened her eyes. They were dilated and she looked through him.

"You're just having a few side effects from the medication." He glanced over his shoulder at the doctor. "Dr. Galen is making the necessary adjustments."

"Headache," she wheezed.

"Don't talk. Just lie still and relax." He stood and turned to the doctor. "Test her blood. That should tell you if you've overmedicated her. I recognize the symptoms. I have everything you need in the supply room."

When Cyrus and Dr. Galen stepped out into the hall, Johanna could hear that they had stopped outside the door to discuss her condition. If he was in the hall then he wasn't anywhere close to the camera that continued to watch over her through the air vent.

She had a skull-splitting headache, and she was wheezing like a ninety-year-old man in a snoring frenzy. But as long as she could think clearly she would continue the risky plan. Quickly she picked up the inhaler off the nightstand and sucked in another oral dose of albuterol, then repeated it twice more.

Too much of a good thing for an asthmatic could be toxic, but there was no way she was going to let Cyrus touch her, even if it meant playing a dangerous game with her medication levels.

Actually, she was achieving two things at the same time. In her condition he couldn't make love to her, and her erratic health kept him distracted from focusing on Adolf. As he had told her earlier, she was his weakness, and she intended to use that against him now.

She didn't want to put Dr. Galen's life in jeopardy. He'd been in and out of the room frantically trying to figure out why she wasn't stabilizing. But Cyrus wasn't going to kill him—he was too worried about keeping her alive.

When the door opened she closed her eyes and exhaled a painful wheeze. She heard footsteps. It was the doctor. She could smell his unusual scent. She felt a needle pierce her arm. Heard Cyrus say, "When can she be moved, Galen?"

"I wouldn't advise it until she's stabilized."

"Then get to it. We reach the island in two hours, and I want her off the yacht."

"I don't think she'll be stable by then. Maybe tomorrow. I'll get her medication regulated and we'll pray it works."

"You pray. Pray hard. If God doesn't answer and she's not on her feet by tomorrow, I'll answer for Him with a bullet between your eyes."

When the door closed and she knew they had both walked out again, Johanna opened her eyes and reached for her inhaler. If she kept it up she could die, but if she was forced to sleep with Cyrus she would want to die anyway.

Two more times, Johanna thought, as she sucked hard on the inhaler, then quickly put it back on the nightstand.

The *Aldora* had drifted again, this time a hundred yards from where Sly and Sully had found her days ago. The rain had stopped, but the black sky was still threatening.

Wearing scuba gear, Merrick and Sly moved through the rubble and headed for the galley. The fire had sent the *Aldora* to the bottom of the sea, but it hadn't destroyed her underbelly. That was good news, Merrick thought as he motioned to Sly, then swam through the debris and into the galley. He saw the cupboard wasn't entirely intact, but he'd fastened the waterproof canister to the ceiling of a bottom cupboard with a powerful magnet.

On a number of missions they'd used a dead-letter box to transfer information from one agent to his contact without detection. Days ago Merrick had used a DLB to stash his phone equipped with a GPS for safekeeping.

At the time he had picked Johanna up in Hora, he'd believed she was *happy* with Cyrus. If that had turned out to be true, as much as he would have hated using her, he would have given her back Cyrus's ring and allowed her to escape in hopes of tracking her on the GPS to Cyrus's hideout.

He wasn't proud of the fact that he had doubted her, but today he was damn glad he hadn't let his emotions blindside his training.

Now he only hoped that the ring was on the move instead of still around Holic's dead guard's neck blasting a signal from the shepherd's cottage in the hills.

He ran his hand inside the cupboard and surprised a small leopard shark taking a nap. The shark shot out of the cupboard over Merrick's right shoulder, knocked Sly back six feet and headed through the maze of ruins for the open sea.

Sly motioned he was all right and, undeterred, Merrick slid his hand into the left front corner of the cupboard and locked his hand around the waterproof three-inch-long canister. Pulling it free from the magnet, he zipped the DLB into his tactical belt, then followed Sly back out of the wreckage.

On board the *Marina*, Merrick pulled off his goggles and pulled the canister from his belt. He glanced at his men, all standing around him now, hoping for the same thing he was—that Cyrus had found the ring and that they'd have a moving signal.

He pulled out the phone and turned it on. The screen lit up. Then he turned on the GPS. A map materialized.

A flashing red dot started to move.

"Pride and ego," Merrick said. "We've got him."

Johanna woke up and realized that the inhaler on the nightstand was gone, that the *Starina* was no longer moving and whatever Dr. Galen had done to stabilize her erratic breathing had turned her incessant ragged wheezing into a soft, almost nonexistent whistle. Her headache was gone, too.

The doctor was sitting on the couch watching her with his arms crossed over his chest. His dark eyes told her that he knew she had purposely aggravated her condition—the reason her inhaler was no longer in reach.

He wasn't a big man, and he looked over sixty, his hair long for a man his age and in his profession. She glanced at the wall vent, and he followed her gaze.

"He's on the island," he said.

"And my son?"

"He's with him."

"Guards?"

"Six that I've seen. The others went ashore with him. Is he your husband?"

"No. If he told you that, he's lying."

"You could have died, you know."

Johanna sat up slowly. She was no longer hooked up to the intravenous theophylline. "Does he know I've been stabilized?"

"Not yet."

"Don't tell him."

He stood and walked to the bed. "He's threatened my life. I either save yours or mine is over."

"The truth is, Dr. Galen, once you save my life, yours is definitely over. You won't leave here alive once I'm no longer at death's door. So, if I were you, I would at least make it look as if I still need you."

His eyes widened as he considered what she was saying. "You believe that?"

"With all my heart. So, what do you say, Doctor? Do you want to live a while longer or die before breakfast?"

"How long do you think you can fool him?"

"That depends on you. Be convincing."

"I won't let you die," he promised. "I'll figure out something."

Johanna reached out and squeezed the doctor's hand. "Keep that worried look on your face. He's very smart." Then she closed her eyes and started to simulate the obnoxious wheezing that signaled she was still in distress.

* * *

The GPS stopped moving and continued to flash on an island south of Corfu. Paxi was the smallest islet in the Ionian Sea, virtually unspoiled, and the west coast was lined with rugged cliffs. It was just the kind of desolation Cyrus was known for, and it was here that Merrick would find Johanna.

If they were lucky they would be able to strike before dawn.

Dressed in black, the sheen of their faces smudged with camo paint, under the cover of night, the Rat Fighters began to prepare for their siege. Merrick had given his last instruction as Ash Kelly had killed the *Marina*'s engine a mile offshore and dropped anchor.

Sly studied the island's typography on his computer. "He's in a sea cave," he said. "His hideout is built right into the damn thing. It's going to be a bitch getting in there." He pointed to a long channel. "If we dock here it'll take us another two hours to reach the cave. It will be daylight by then. It's either that or we swim from here. In that case, Ash stays here to pick us up."

"I don't like that," Ash grumbled.

"I don't either," Merrick said. "We need everyone active." He pointed to the sea cave. "There's an opening in the cave's ceiling. We can rappel down. If things go to hell it'll be our way out."

Sly nodded. "Then head for this shoreline, Ash, and watch out for rocks. The surf is going to send us into shore like a hurricane's on our ass."

The *Marina* proved to be a gutsy little cruiser, and Ash Kelly's expertise guided her into shore. It took a long hour to maneuver on the rocks once they started out on foot. Merrick led the way, and he never looked back, his mind focused only on Johanna and his son.

They found the open hole in the roof of the cave, and rappelled down like sea pirates after stolen booty. Finding a rock as cover, Merrick motioned to the *Starina* and the guards that were still on board.

"What do you make of that?" Pierce whispered.

"They're guarding something on the boat," Bjorn said.

"Maybe he's not planning on staying long. Maybe this is just a stop-off on his way somewhere else."

"Then I say we find out what's on board," Pierce said. "Merrick, what do you say?"

Merrick pulled the GPS from his pocket. "That ring is on the yacht," he said. "I say Johanna is, too."

"And the boy?" Sly asked.

"I don't know. We take out the guards. No gunfire. Nobody dies." Merrick got confused looks from all his men. "I don't want us mistaking my son for one of those guards. Bound and gagged," he ordered, "then knock out the yacht's twin engines so she's dead in the water. Any surveillance equipment. I'll find Johanna."

They split up. Pierce, Ash and Bjorn slipped into the water, and Sly and Merrick took a rocky grade that sloped down to the pier.

The guards never knew what hit them. No shots fired, no noise, just sickening thuds as six bodies slumped to the *Starina's* deck. Then, while Pierce and Bjorn tied up the men, Sly and Ash went below to find the engine room.

Merrick was moving down the companionway when he came upon a short stocky guard. Not Erik, he thought, then drove the butt of his MP-5 into the man's face, eased him to the floor before he snapped his neck.

The yacht was big, and he silently moved down the hall opening up doors. He saw the double door at the end of the hall and knew it was Cyrus's stateroom. He had no idea if he was on board. He moved to the door, listened.

Nothing.

He went in hard and fast, his gun out in front. He startled a man on the couch and swung the gun at him, but before he drilled him, Johanna said, "Don't shoot him, Adolf."

He jerked his head toward the bed and knew immediately

that something was wrong. Johanna was wearing a white satin robe, and her skin looked paper-white. He saw that her arm was turned over, palm up, and that there was a needle feeding her some kind of drug.

"Asthma attack?" he asked.

"Yes."

"You all right now?"

"Yes."

"Sit," he told the wide-eyed Greek, and as the man dropped back on the couch with his hands raised high, Merrick backed around the bed with his gun still leveled at the man's chest. "Can you walk?" he asked Johanna.

"Yes. How did you find me?"

Merrick glanced at her hand. He'd been right. Cyrus had found the ring and it was back on Johanna's finger. "Long story." He motioned to the man on the sofa who looked as if fear had paralyzed him. "Who's he?"

"A doctor from Kárpathos City. I had the attack there. The doctor saved my life. Don't kill him, Adolf. He deserves to get out of here alive. That's all he wants."

"Don't move," Merrick said to the man. *"Katalaveno?"*
The man nodded. "I speak English. I sit right here."

Merrick relaxed his arm and slid his finger off the trigger; the MP-5 stayed at his side. Johanna had sat up and she pulled the tape away from the needle in her arm. Only it wasn't in her arm. The tape hid the fact that it was simply lying on her skin. "What's that all about?" he asked.

"Long story," she said, giving his words back to him. "I'll explain later." She climbed out of the bed and flattened herself against him and hugged him, burying her face against his chest. "I'm sorry I left Aperi," she said, "but Cyrus threatened to hurt Erik, and—"

"Shh…" Merrick wrapped his arm around her and hugged her with one arm. Then he lifted her chin and said, "I acted like an ass."

"I should have told you sooner."

"We've made some mistakes. Both of us. Where's Erik?"

"I think he's with Cyrus."

"Have you ever been here before?"

"I haven't left the yacht since it docked. Where are we?"

"Paxi."

She frowned. "No. I've never been here."

"True to form," Merrick said. "The bastard's always got one more surprise in his pocket."

"Get your hands off her."

Merrick jerked his head up and saw a black-haired young man standing in the doorway. It was the first time he had laid eyes on his son. The situation could have been better. Erik's hand was wrapped around a Glock aimed straight at him.

"I said let her go!"

Johanna dropped her arms from around Adolf's waist and slowly fit herself in front of him. "Erik, put down the gun."

"What are you doing, Mom? Get over here."

"No."

"No?"

She knew she was confusing him, but she wasn't going to move. He would shoot Adolf the minute she did. "Put the gun down, Erik. You can't shoot him."

"I can, and I'm going to. The guards are gone. Probably dead in the water. There's one in the hall. He killed him, and he's here to kill us."

"You're wrong. He came here to save us."

Erik shook his head. "That's crazy. You're crazy. Get away from him now."

"Johanna, do what he says."

"Johanna?" Erik looked at Adolf, then back at her. "What did he call you?"

"Erik, put the gun down, and I'll explain."

"Explain what?"

"My name isn't Callia. It's…Johanna Merrick."

He frowned. "Merrick?"

"Probably not the best time to tell him that," Adolf said.

"There is no good time, Adolf." Johanna reached out to her son. "Give me the gun, Erik."

He stood there a minute, then his face turned angrier than ever. "You went to Naxos to be with him, didn't you?"

"That's not how it happened, but I'm glad I went. Erik, it's very complicated, and I'll tell you everything, but you need to give me the gun."

"Move away, Mom." Erik raised the gun a little higher. Aimed at Adolf's head.

"Erik, no!"

Adolf asked, "How good a shot is he?"

"I don't know," Johanna answered.

Merrick swore. "Then do what he says. Move away. If I have to shoot him, I won't kill him."

She glanced over her shoulder. "What are you saying?"

"Dammit, Johanna, do what I tell you."

If she moved Erik would shoot his father, or Adolf would shoot his son. There was no way she was going to let that happen. "I'm not going anywhere, and nobody is going to shoot anyone. Erik—"

He fired the gun. It all happened in less than a second. Adolf shoved her onto the bed and as she fell, her eyes widened when Adolf was knocked backward off his feet.

"No!" She scrambled to her feet and ran to him, dropped down on her knees. "Oh, God…"

"Get away from him, Mom!"

She turned and glared at her son. "If you want to kill him, you're going to have to kill me first, Erik."

Sly heard the gun blast from the engine room and looked at Ash. "That wasn't Merrick's gun. Finish up here, and then find Bjorn and Pierce. I'm going after him."

Sly left the engine room and headed down the hall. He heard voices. Johanna was telling her son to put down the gun. He must have been the one who had fired the shot.

He reached the bend in the hall and clung close to the wall, peeked around the corner. He saw a young man standing in an open doorway, a Glock in his hand. He was ten feet away.

He flattened his back against the wall again. "Merrick!"

"Sly, don't shoot him," Merrick yelled from inside the room.

Sly peeked around the corner again, and the kid spun around and fired down the hall. Sly ducked back. He heard Merrick swear. Sly looked around the corner in time to see Merrick sailing through the air and knocking Erik off his feet. He came around the corner fast and kicked the gun out of Erik's hand, then picked it up.

Merrick came to his feet, pulling Erik up with him.

Sly saw that Merrick had taken a hit in his right shoulder. "The kid do that?"

"Well, I didn't shoot myself." He gave Erik a push toward the couch, then said, "Get out of here, doc. Sly, he goes with us when we pull out. Those shots no doubt gave us up. Warn the men, and get back here as quick as you can."

When the doctor scrambled to his feet and out the door, Merrick slammed it behind him. From outside in the hall, Sly heard Merrick say to his son, "Sit down, you little son of a bitch."

Merrick glared at his son. "I said, nail your ass to that couch before I knock you off your feet."

"Adolf, please…"

Merrick glanced at Johanna. "You all right?"

"The question is, are you?"

"I'll live."

She headed into the bathroom and came back out with a handful of towels. "Take off your shirt."

He didn't. Staring at Erik, he reached up, grabbed the shoulder seam of his fitted black long-sleeve T-shirt and ripped it off.

He heard her say "The bullet went through," as she folded a towel around his shoulder and added pressure. "That's good, right? That's what you said before."

He glanced at her. She was crying and that was making it harder for her to breathe.

She looked up at him. "That's good, right?"

Then he reach around and swept a strand of hair away from her shoulder. "It's good, honey."

"That's touching. A killer and his whore having a moment."

Merrick swore, then tossed the towel to the floor and in two long strides reached Erik, grabbed the front of his shirt and picked him up off the couch.

Johanna cried out. "Adolf, stop!"

He ignored her and swung Erik up against the wall. Pinned him there. "Never speak to your mother like that again," he growled.

"Adolf, he's just upset."

He felt Johanna behind him, tugging on the back of his shirt. He backed off, let Erik go. Said, "That makes two of us."

"Erik, Cyrus told you all kinds of lies. You have to listen to me."

"You're the liar, Mom."

Merrick bit back the urge to slam the kid's head into the wall and knock some sense into him. Instead, he said, "Your mother has spent twenty years living a lie to save your ass. Everything she's done has been for you." He stepped back, looked at Johanna. "You going to tell him, or do you want me to?"

The look on her face was pure agony. Then she glanced at Erik and said, "You're right. I have lied to you, but no more. Cyrus isn't your father, Erik. This is your father. If you look at him, really look, you'll know I'm telling the truth."

The kid shook his head. "That's a lie."

"I have no reason to lie anymore." Then much softer, she said, "I love you, and—"

An explosion rocked the *Starina.* It sent Johanna and Erik to the floor, and Merrick off balance. He heard the bulkhead splintering and then water was rushing into the stateroom.

He moved like lightning, scooping up Johanna and tossing her onto the bed. "Hang on to that iron post," he instructed.

The words were barely out of his mouth when the yacht began listing hard. Erik was back on his feet, and Merrick reached out and pulled him toward the statue of Zeus. "Get a good grip, she's going over." Then he pitched himself toward the bed. Johanna was off it now, holding tight on to the iron post as the big yacht began to roll, laying the gunwale horizontal to the water.

Merrick grabbed the iron bedpost with his good arm at the same time he jammed his foot against the post low along the floor. It brought him around quickly and he reached out with his other hand and gripped the post, pinning Johanna between him and the iron to keep her from being washed away.

He glanced back at Erik. "Don't let go!" he yelled.

The *Starina* groaned as she came to rest on her side, then the lights went out.

Chapter 13

"Merrick!"

Merrick heard Sly call out to him, then saw the beam of a flashlight. "We're here," he called back

"Erik?" Johanna's voice was half-strength. "Erik!"

"I'm all right," he finally said.

"We lose anyone, Sly?" Merrick yelled.

"Pierce took a bullet, but you know him. He's like you. Takes more than one to drop him. Cyrus's second siege of guards are down."

"Cyrus?"

"Haven't seen him."

"Get my son out of here. I'll meet you on the pier. If it's still there."

"She's standing."

Merrick heard Sly say to Erik, "Let go, kid. I've got you." He turned his attention to Johanna. "I got you, too, honey. You can let go of the post now."

She let go, and he wrapped his arm around her waist and they began to swim in the direction he'd seen the light beam when Sly had showed up.

Twenty minutes later, Merrick was standing on the pier with Johanna clinging to him and Erik glaring at him. Then his son made his move. He reached around Sly, grabbed his gun, then took off running toward the rock acropolis that Cyrus had built into the sea cave.

"Erik!" Johanna pulled away from him and started after her son. Merrick reached out and hauled her back. "Give me the ring."

She looked at him as if she didn't understand. Merrick grabbed her hand, "The ring."

She slid it off her finger and he pocketed it, then locked eyes with Sly McEwen. "Get her out of here. You have your orders." He looked at Johanna. "Go with my men. I'll bring Erik back."

"Please let me go with you."

"I love you," he said. Then he kissed her and was gone.

The rock hideout was a maze once Merrick got inside, lit by wall sconces. He could hear Erik calling out to Cyrus— to his father.

He followed his son's voice. It was growing more frantic in his efforts to find Cyrus. Merrick sprinted through another corridor, up a series of steps. He knew Cyrus had a submarine, thought he would use it now to elude capture, but Erik was going up, not down.

He kept moving. Another corridor, then another. Then he heard Cyrus's voice as he came around a corner. He jerked to a stop and stepped back, flattening himself against the wall.

"He's got Mom."

"Don't worry, Erik. Merrick is outnumbered. The men will—"

"They're all dead. He brought men with him."

"How many?"

"I saw four."

"He brought the Rat Fighters with him."

"The what?"

"Never mind." Cyrus swore. "How the hell did he find me so quick?"

"What about Mom?"

"She'll come to me. You're here. She won't go anywhere without you."

"I saw her with him."

"Merrick?"

"Yes. Before the explosion. I was with her. She told me…"

"What did she tell you?"

"That you're not my father. That's a lie, right?"

"Of course it's a lie. How did you get away?" Cyrus asked.

"After we made it off the yacht, I just ran."

"That means Merrick is not far behind. This isn't the way I planned it. No, not exactly, but it will work. Perhaps even better."

"Planned what? What are you doing?"

"I'm getting ready to receive my guest. Knowing Merrick as well as I do, he's sent Callia off the island with his men, and he'll be here soon."

Merrick stepped around a pillar and into a high-domed cave. "Sooner than you think."

"Not really. Your timing is perfect. Hello, old buddy."

Erik had spun around. "Where's my mother?"

"Like he said, she's on her way off the island," Merrick answered.

"Father?"

"Not to worry, Erik. I'll have her back soon. Very soon. Shoot him, Erik," Cyrus said. "Kill him."

Merrick saw the smile on Cyrus's face. He said, "He shoots me and then you shoot him, or were you planning for me to shoot him in a volley of gunfire?"

Cyrus's smile widened. "Why would I do that?"

"Because he's not your son."

"Sad, but true. The game is, who is faster? You see, I've been training him, Merrick. He's not as fast as you, but he has your raw instincts for survival."

"I won't shoot my son, Cyrus." Merrick glanced at Erik and the look on his face was pure horror. "Step away, Erik."

His son stood frozen. "She was telling me the truth. You're my father."

"It's the truth. I'm your father," Merrick said.

Cyrus pulled a gun from his pocket. "A sad reunion for you both, but one I've been envisioning for years. My plan, however, was to have you kill him first, then find out you'd killed your own son. But perhaps this plan is better. Watching him die at my hand should bring back a few memories."

Erik backed up, but he was still too far away for Merrick to reach him in time. He stalled. "Have you figured it out yet?"

Cyrus's smiled slipped a little. "Figured out what?"

"Don't you want to know how I found you?"

"I admit I'm curious."

Erik backed up another foot.

A few more feet son, Merrick thought. *Come on. Keep moving.*

"It was the ring," he said. "Here." He slowly slid his hand into his pocket and pulled it out. Tossed it to Cyrus.

Cyrus caught it. "You put a tracking device in it. You son of a bitch. You were always a slippery bastard. But it hardly matters now. I was going to call you, anyway. Of course, my hope was that you'd bring Melita with you in exchange for your family. No chance of that, I suppose?"

"No chance."

"How is my little bitch?"

"I've decided to adopt her," Merrick taunted. "She's won my heart, and my protection. When I arrived in Greece she was the one who opened my eyes. She saw a picture of Johanna and told me it was Callia. That they were one and the same."

"There's still the question as to how you lured Callia away from Corfu."

"Zeta Poulos. You left her daughter in Hora. That was sloppy."

"Again I applaud your efforts, but it falls short. The game is over and it's time for me to collect the prize. And I will get Callia back. It's only a matter of time. Melita, too."

Merrick saw Cyrus's eyes shift to Erik. He didn't think. Didn't hesitate. He lunged at his son; at the same time he raised the MP-5 strapped to his side and fired. Cyrus fired, too. Twice.

He heard Erik groan, but as he went down, his son made a valiant effort to stay focused. He fired his gun at Cyrus and although it went wide, it surprised Cyrus and prevented him from firing another shot. Taken off his game, Cyrus darted into a tunnel behind him and suddenly he was gone.

Merrick leapt to his feet and glanced at Erik. Saw the blood on his arm. "How bad is it?"

"How the hell should I know! I've never been shot before."

Merrick grabbed ahold of his son's arm. "The bullet just grazed you."

"You're bleeding bad."

Merrick glanced at his shoulder. Cyrus had shot him in the same damn shoulder Erik had earlier. "Get your ass back to the pier." He tossed Erik his phone with the GPS. "Call Sly—he'll come back for you. Where does that tunnel go?"

"To the top. He's got a helicopter up there."

The tunnel sloped steadily upward, and as Merrick sprinted through it he could feel a cool breeze moving. He came out of the tunnel just as he heard the helicopter engine begin to sing. He raised his gun and blasted a dozen rounds into the side of the iron bird. Cyrus went out the door on the other side, fired back and then sprinted to the cliffs seconds before the helicopter's fuel tank blew and the bird lit up the sky in a ball of flames.

Merrick was blown back off his feet. Dazed for several minutes, he lay there unable to get up. When he could think again, he scanned the rocky cliff and saw Cyrus in the distance on foot. He forced himself to his feet and headed after him. The bastard probably had a boat hidden somewhere.

Merrick raced along the rocky cliff after Cyrus, trying to keep him in his sight. He followed him for an hour at an agonizing pace. He was gaining on him, but Cyrus had a good head start.

He kept moving, determined. Thirty minutes later Cyrus came to a stop, and Merrick realized he'd trapped himself—he was on the edge of a cliff that led nowhere but straight down.

He turned to face Merrick. Out of breath, he said, "Game on. Your move."

For an answer Merrick charged him and forced Cyrus to the ground. He threw a hard punch to his jaw, and Cyrus retaliated with one just as violent. Punches flying, like two pit bulls in a fight to the death, the clash was brutal. Surrender wasn't an option—neither one intended to lose.

Back and forth, strength and rage—over twenty years of hate—driving them on and on, and on and on.

Cyrus slammed his fist into Merrick's gut, then kneed him in the groin. He broke free and scrambled to his feet, then kicked Merrick in the ribs.

"When you're dead, I'm going to find them, Merrick. I'm going to kill your seed, and take Callia that same night. I'm going to live your life with her." Another hard kick. "You'll hear her moaning in my bed from hell."

Merrick grabbed Cyrus's foot on the next kick and twisted it hard, throwing him off balance. Cyrus went down hard, rolled to his side, and the fight continued.

Like crazed animals, they pummeled each other over and over again until neither one realized they had run out of ground. Then momentum and rage took them, and they were falling off the rocky cliff plunging sixty feet into the sea.

Johanna saw the shoreline of Amorgós with the dawn. She sat numb, wrapped in a blanket as the *Marina* headed for a lonely pier. She'd refused to go below. Refused to look at Sly McEwen. He'd told her that he was following orders. Adolf had one goal and that was keeping her alive. If their plan went sour, Sly was to take charge of Johanna's safety.

He was a man much like her husband. Efficient, determined and loyal. He would carry out Adolf's orders no matter what. Even if he didn't like them.

That had been evident by the look on his face when they had reached the boat in the cove and an explosion had lit up the highest cliff on Paxi.

She had pleaded with him to go back. She had seen in his eyes that he wanted to, but he'd simply said, "I have my orders."

But he had sent Bjorn Odell and Pierce Fourtier back to Cyrus's compound. He'd been in contact with them twice, but as of yet, they hadn't been able to find anyone. Not alive, or dead.

As Ash Kelly steered the *Marina* into the bay, Johanna saw a man standing on the pier. *This must be Sully Paxton*, she thought. Tall, with black hair and intense eyes, the iron man grabbed the line Sly McEwen tossed him and tied up the boat.

"You hear anything yet?" he asked.

Sly glanced at her, then back at Sully. He shook his head, obviously not wanting to upset her.

Sully's eyes shifted to her, then he held out his hand. "Come on, Johanna. We'll get you into the house. Melita is waiting."

She had expected his voice to be as rough and hard as he looked. But his husky voice had an Irish accent and was as gentle as a breeze. No wonder Melita had found solace in it.

Still angry at Sly McEwen, she stood and, keeping the blanket wrapped around her, let Sully help her out of the boat. When he saw she was shoeless he moved to pick her up, but Sly McEwen had followed her off the boat and scooped her up in his powerful arms.

"I can walk," she insisted.

"I know you can, but your breathing has been erratic since we left Paxi."

"Maybe that's because you deserted my husband and son," she argued.

He didn't like what she'd said. His jaw jerked and he started toward the house on the hill, barking an order at Ash Kelly to fill Sully in on *the plan.*

"What plan?" she asked, halfway up the hill.

"I have my orders."

The door swung open and Melita's beautiful face was all Johanna could see. Sly set her on her feet, and then Melita stepped forward. "Please don't hate me," she said, "I didn't know."

An hour later, after a shower, and wearing Melita's clothes, Johanna stood at the bedroom window and stared out over the bay. The waiting was pure agony.

They should have heard something by now. Sly McEwen was avoiding her, and perhaps that was because he knew something he didn't think she was strong enough to handle.

Were they dead? All of them?

A knock on the door sent her away from the window. "Come in."

The door opened and Melita came in carrying a tray. "I brought you tea and something to eat."

"I'm not hungry, but thank you anyway."

"I know this probably isn't the right time, but I…"

"I don't blame you, Melita, and I could never hate you. From what Adolf told me you've been a victim as much as I have."

"If only that made me feel better."

"You're safe now."

She nodded. "Thanks to Sully."

"You love him?"

"Yes."

"And does he love you?"

"Yes."

"Then hold on to that, and live, Melita. Live your life with Sully, and don't look back."

"Simon's dead."

"Yes, I know. Adolf told me. I'm sorry."

"He's here. Sully brought his ashes to me. Simon loved the sea and so I set him free here."

The pain on Melita's face drew Johanna across the room. She hugged her, and said, "The only good thing to come out of this is you." She pulled back, brushed Melita's long black hair away from her face. "I've always seen you as my daughter, even though we never got to spend much time together."

It was then that Johanna heard Sly McEwen's voice. He'd come back into the house, and she looked up as he appeared in the bedroom doorway. If he had news it wasn't good. His mood seemed to be even more sour than when he had dumped her on Melita's doorstep.

"What's happened?"

"Bjorn and Pierce called in. They reached the explosion sight and the wreckage."

"Wreckage?"

"It was a helicopter. It looks like it blew up before it got a chance to take off."

"What does that mean?"

"I have my orders," Sly said. "Get ready to leave."

"Leave and go where?"

"Washington. My orders are to escort you back to Washington. We leave within the hour."

"I'm not leaving Greece," Johanna snapped. "I'm not going

anywhere until I know if my husband and son are dead or alive."

"I have my orders, and if I have to tie you up and carry you, I will. If Merrick and your son are alive, then the men will find them. Sully and Ash are leaving to head back to Paxi. I'd like to be in on that search, but Merrick put you in my hands and the last thing I intend to do is go against his wishes. Melita, Sully told me to tell you that you'll be going with him. He wants you down on the pier in ten minutes."

Merrick thought it was the sun warming his face that had roused him, but it was a voice that had jerked him awake.

"I thought you were dead."

The relief in his son's voice as Erik crouched down beside him pulled Merrick out of his pain. Blood loss and a sixty-foot drop into the sea had drained him, and every muscle in his body protested as he pulled himself up and sat forward.

"I thought I told you to get off the island."

"I thought you might need my help." Erik glanced toward the beach. "He's not dead."

Merrick frowned. "What?"

Erik motioned to where Cyrus's body lay on the beach. "I was looking for you all night. At dawn I found him."

The tide must have washed him ashore, Merrick thought. They had plunged into the water together, but the current had separated them. He'd dragged himself to an outcropping of rocks and he must have passed out.

He pulled himself up, and when his knee buckled Erik stood quickly and grabbed him to keep him on his feet. Merrick looked up and saw the truth in his son's eyes. They were bloodshot and weary from combing the treacherous cliffs throughout the night.

"I saw you fall," he admitted. "I thought when I found you, you'd be dead."

"I dislocated my knee," Merrick said. "Help me down to him."

Together they moved slowly over the rocky terrain to where Cyrus was stretched out on the beach. If he wasn't dead, he was certainly in bad shape. He hadn't moved.

As they reached the beach, Merrick stopped and said, "Wait here." Then on his own power, limping heavily, he moved toward Cyrus. When he stood over him, Cyrus's eyes shifted and looked up at him. He hadn't moved. Not even his head.

"Another place, a different time, but it holds a familiar memory, wouldn't you say? Me on my back, and you looking down at a wounded comrade."

"You're not my comrade—you're the enemy," Merrick said.

"Comrade…enemy. You hold the power now, just like you did that night in that minefield in Prague. How does it feel to hold it again, Merrick? To hold my life in your hands?"

He was so damn still that Merrick knew something wasn't right. No movement at all, just his eyes. But he was lucid. He bent down and did a quick assessment of Cyrus's body. He was fifty-eight, built like a field soldier.

No blood. No evidence of any kind of injury that would keep him down, except for one. He reached out and put his hand on Cyrus's leg. Cyrus didn't feel it, and that's when Merrick knew the fall had severed something vital. No doubt his spinal column.

Cyrus was paralyzed.

"It's time," Cyrus said. "It's time for you to do what you should have done in Prague. Kill me, Merrick. Kill me now. I can't move. Do what you should have done years ago. Kill me."

Merrick pulled himself to his feet. He glanced at Erik and, when their eyes locked, his son started to walk toward him. "What's wrong with him?"

"He's paralyzed."

Erik glanced down at Cyrus. "Will he live?"

The question hung in the air for several seconds, then Merrick limped away.

"Merrick! Come back here, you son of a bitch! You owe me. This time get it right! Merrick! Come back here, you bastard. Kill me. Kill me!"

Cyrus's curses and guttural screams followed Merrick as he moved to a crag jutting out over the sea. He stood weary in body and mind, the wind in his face. Cyrus was still screaming at him, competing with the wind and the crashing of the waves against the rocks.

Merrick wanted to shut him up. To kill him. To kill him for Johanna, and for all the years he had kept him from his son. It had been his primary goal from the moment he'd learned that Johanna was alive. But Onyxx's goal was broader based, and Harry Pendleton had reminded him the day he left Washington that this was bigger than a personal war.

Cyrus Krizova was only one piece of a very big puzzle. He had hideouts and monastery prisons scattered all over Greece. Who else knew about them? How many other men were out there buried in the bowels of monastery prisons, as Sully had been until a few months ago? How many lives were hanging on to the fragile hope of being rescued? How many wives were waiting to hear whether their husbands were still alive?

"What does he mean, you owe him?"

Erik had come up behind him. "I'll tell you about it someday. Right now I need to let the men know where to find us. Give me the phone I gave you back at the hideout." When Erik hesitated, Merrick turned to look at his son. "I said—"

"I lost it. It must have fallen out of my pocket while I was searching the cliffs for you. Are you going to kill him?"

"Not today, Erik. Not today."

By late afternoon the weather had turned sour and the hard-hitting wind had forced Merrick and Erik to drag Cyrus off the beach. In the shelter of a grotto, listening to Cyrus cursing him, Merrick reached down and gave his own knee a hard jerk.

He swallowed the pain of putting his dislocated knee back in place, then glanced up to see Erik watching him.

"What did you do?"

"Realigned my knee. Old injury."

"Hell, that must have hurt."

"Not any more than being shot twice in the same shoulder."

Erik settled on a rock across from him. "I'm sorry. I didn't believe that—"

"I'm your father?"

"I do now. Hell, we kind of look alike."

Merrick had noticed that.

"Do you think your men will find us?"

Merrick, bare from the waist up, pulled his knife from his boot and sliced into the side seam of his black pullover. "They'll find us sooner or later."

"What are you going to do with that?"

Merrick cut a narrow strip, then stood. "I'm going to stuff this piece in his mouth to shut him up, then I'm going to climb out on the ledge above us and find a sharp rock to fly us a flag. Get some sleep."

The grotto turned quiet after that and Merrick found a rock where he secured his shirt. Back inside, he found Erik still awake.

He bedded down and studied his son. Johanna had given him a son. The boy had a lot to learn, but he was determined and he had guts.

Erik looked over at him. "Did you fly the flag?"

"She's flying. When you see your mother, I expect you to apologize to her."

Erik hung his head. "She lied to me."

"To save your life. Next time you get the urge to spit fire, you come at me. Not her. If you do it again, I'll knock you on your ass. Now, get some sleep."

Early morning Merrick woke up to the familiar sound of a boat engine. He stepped out into the sunlight, looked up and saw that his black flag was still flying. The damn wind was good for something, at least.

He limped down to the beach as Sully Paxton's cruiser slowed, and the Irishman showed off his gun-running talents by maneuvering the boat into shore, dancing around the rocks as if he were doing the two-step with his lover.

Merrick saw that Melita was with him, and Ash. Sully dropped anchor, then leapt out of the cruiser into the water. He said something to Melita. She nodded and stayed where she was while Sully and Ash came ashore.

Ash called out, "That pirate flag yours, captain?" He was grinning ear to ear.

For an answer, Merrick said, "What the hell took you so long?"

Sully's grin topped Ash's. "We decided to give Melita a tour of the island's coast. Been around it twice." He looked up to the high, jagged cliff. "How the hell did you end up on this side of the island?"

"Later." When Sully looked past Merrick to the entrance of the grotto, he turned around to see Erik standing there. "That's my son. How's Johanna?"

"Mad as a killer bee," Ash said. "Sly flew her back to Washington yesterday afternoon. That was your order. My bet is he had to tie her in the seat on the plane. I wouldn't want to be your ass when she lays eyes on you again."

Merrick grinned. He'd told Sly if the mission went sour, Johanna's safety came first. Hers and Erik's. By rights, Erik should have been on that plane with her.

"When I saw the flag I phoned Bjorn and Pierce," Ash said. "They've been searching the island on foot since we took off with Johanna back to Amorgós. We'll pick them up on the other side of the island. Come on, kid," Ash hollered. "Let's go."

"Not yet," Merrick said. "We've got another passenger. Cyrus is inside."

Ash and Sully looked at each other. Then Sully said, "Is he dead or alive?"

"Alive. If you can call it that. Let's load him in the boat."

Cyrus started screaming the minute Merrick removed the gag from his mouth. He continued to curse Merrick to hell as Sully and Ash carried him to the cruiser. He fell silent the minute he saw Melita standing on the deck with her arm around Erik. It wasn't the reunion Cyrus had hoped for, Merrick thought.

He saw Melita raise her chin and, like a protective sister, pull Erik closer. She didn't say a word to her father, then Cyrus was carried down the companionway and into the stateroom.

Cyrus lay on the bed and waited. She would come to him. Melita would come. She was his only hope. She would come.

He waited until the sun through the window no longer lit the room. Waited until he began to grind his teeth. When he was about to give up on her, he heard the door open.

The light came on and then Melita was beside the bed with a tray in her hand. She said, "I've come to feed you."

"I don't want food, you little bitch. What I want from you now is only one thing."

"And what would that be?"

"For you to kill me."

She set the tray on the nightstand. Sat down on the bed next to him. "I'm not a killer. That's who you are, not me. You torture and destroy. I told you once before, I will never be like you."

"This is no life."

"Finally we agree on something."

"Then do it now before Merrick comes."

"You misunderstand. I agree that being a prisoner is no

life. I've been one, remember? Your prisoner all my life. You feel trapped. Helpless. Frightened. Do you feel all those things? Are you capable of any emotion besides hate?"

Cyrus was livid. "I'm your father. I order you to kill me."

"I brought you some soup and a straw. If you refuse it, you'll be fed intravenously." Her eyes drifted over his useless body. "I'll come back to feed you. I see that you've soiled yourself. I'll send someone down to clean you up."

He'd pissed his pants and hadn't even known he'd done it. Humiliated, Cyrus closed his eyes and began to pray for God to end his life. When the door opened again it was Merrick who came into his line of vision.

"Melita told me you pissed yourself."

"If you didn't come to kill me, get out."

"It would be inhumane for me to let you lie in your own stink."

"Don't touch me."

"You won't feel a thing. Sorry. Poor joke."

"You owe me, Merrick. Kill me."

"My men will be transporting you to Prague. Lev Polax at EURO-Quest has agreed to take over the recovery mission and wrap up, should you agree to give up the names of your associates and the locations of your hideouts and prison compounds. Once that is done and verified, I'll honor your wish."

"That will take weeks."

"Maybe months."

Before Merrick left the room he set a tape recorder next to the tray on the nightstand and turned it on. When the door closed, Cyrus stared at his pants behind the door where Merrick had hung them to dry.

Tucked beneath the sheet, disgraced and furious, he started listing names. When he'd finished giving up his associates, he started reciting the locations of every hideout and monastery prison he had tucked away in Greece.

He couldn't die fast enough.

Chapter 14

Johanna had insisted that Sly McEwen take her to the country house. They had been the only words she had spoken to him the entire trip back to Washington. He had agreed and, as he'd left, he had promised her he would notify her the minute he got any news from Greece.

Two hours later he had sent someone from the Agency to deliver an inhaler, nebulizer and a shopping bag to her. Inside she found enough clothes for a week.

She had noticed when the man left that he had pulled down the road and turned off his lights. Sly McEwen was making sure she didn't leave the house. He'd warned her when they had arrived at the airport not to do something stupid. Obviously he was making sure she didn't.

The guard was still there, or perhaps another one had taken his place early in the morning. It was afternoon, and still no word from Greece. Last night she'd been too exhausted and sick at heart to do anything but cry herself to sleep.

In the morning her eyes were swollen and she'd gone into the bathroom to find it the same as she remembered it. From there she'd wandered from room to room, realizing that the house was unchanged. It was as if time had rewound itself.

Her clothes still hung in the closet, and her jewelry box still sat on the vanity. The white curtains were the same, yellowed now with age, but they were the same ones Adolf had helped her hang so long ago.

Johanna found herself in the rose garden and saw that the roses were just beginning to bud. Tears streaming down her cheeks she left the garden, and as she stepped back into the kitchen she spotted the keys on the hook next to the front door. Remembering what they were for, she grabbed them and headed through the side door into the garage. There it was— the white Mustang Adolf had bought her for a wedding present.

She climbed behind the wheel and turned over the engine. It didn't start on the first try, or the second. The third time was the charm, and she hit the button that lifted the garage door and backed out. When she sped past the black sedan parked along the road, the guard stepped out of the woods, zipping up his pants. She looked in the mirror and saw him running to his car, his cell phone already in his hand.

He was calling Sly McEwen.

Johanna pressed her foot down on the gas and lost the Onyxx agent on the second turn. She took the first turn she came to, then the next, remembering the back roads as if she had driven them just yesterday.

She had no idea where she was going; all she knew was that if Adolf and Erik were gone she didn't want to live. She pulled off the road and stopped the car, buried her face in her hands and cried until she couldn't cry anymore. Then she fell asleep behind the wheel of the car.

Johanna woke up to someone tapping on the window. She

jerked awake and saw an elderly man staring at her through the window.

"You all right, lady?"

She buzzed down the window. "I'm fine."

"You sure? You ain't drunk, are you?"

"No."

"Wouldn't blame you if you were. I always have a couple of shots before I come here. I don't like thinkin' about my Edna under all that dirt. Sometimes I hear her begging me to dig her up."

"Excuse me?"

He pointed to the iron gate farther down the road. "You got someone at Oak Hill?"

"Oak Hill… Cemetery?" Johanna opened the car door, forcing the man to step back. She got out and looked past the gate. Last night she hadn't given much thought to where she was. She'd been too upset to care.

She stared at the gate. This was where her grave was. Where Adolf had said Cyrus left roses and that taunting note for him.

"Always come early to visit my Edna," the man said. "Who are you visiting?"

Johanna hadn't planned to go inside, but suddenly she glanced at the old man and said, "Myself." Then she headed for the gate.

She had no idea where to look for the grave, but she passed through the open gate and started down the first narrow path, glancing at the headstones. It was a big cemetery. She didn't realize how big until she had been there for two hours and still hadn't found her grave.

She started down another path and saw a woman with an armful of roses. They were Medallions, the pretty peach petals like velvet in the morning sun.

He left Medallions at your grave.

"Excuse me."

The younger woman turned around. "Yes?"

"Where did you get those roses?"

The woman smiled. "I own a floral shop. I stock them. Finny Floral, if you're interested." She glanced at her watch. "I really need to get these delivered. I have to get to work. I usually don't bring them until after I close, but it's supposed to rain later today."

Johanna watched the woman as she turned down another path. She followed, glancing at headstones. When the woman stopped, she saw her pull wilting Medallions from an ornate cone-shaped vase and place the fresh flowers in it. Then she wrapped the old ones in the paper to dispose of them. Johanna sat down on a bench just off the path. When the woman stepped away from the grave Johanna read the name on the headstone.

JOHANNA MERRICK
BELOVED WIFE
1962–1988

When the woman turned around, Johanna said, "How do you know her?"

The younger woman looked startled to see Johanna sitting on the bench. "I don't. I know her husband."

Johanna frowned. "How do you know Adolf?"

The woman glanced at the grave, then back at Johanna. "Did you know Adolf's wife?"

"Very well. Do you put roses on her grave often?"

"Only when Adolf is out of town, otherwise he brings them himself."

Johanna's heart began to race. She swallowed the lump in her throat. "How long has he been doing that?"

"Since her death. That's why I stock the Medallions. My father and mother used to order them special for him. Since they passed away I've taken over the shop. I make sure there are two dozen Medallions waiting for Adolf every Saturday at four o'clock. That is, unless he's out of town. Then I bring them."

Every Saturday?

"Are you friends?"

The woman hesitated. "Yes...friends."

"Nothing more?" Johanna probed.

"I really don't feel comfortable talking to a stranger about Adolf or his personal business."

"How about his wife?" Johanna said, "would that make a difference?"

It was midmorning when Merrick and Erik landed in Washington. Merrick had called Sly the minute they had been rescued the day before. With flight delays and bad weather, it had taken them longer to get home than he'd planned.

He'd been gnashing his teeth ever since. Sly had confessed that Johanna had ditched her bodyguard and they hadn't been able to find her. He'd called Sly from every airport, and still they hadn't found her.

He rented a car, and he and Erik jumped in. Anxious for an update, he pulled his phone and called Sly. "We just landed. Did you find her?"

"We're still looking. I've been out all night. I went back by the house to leave a man posted there last night. I found the phone I left with her on the kitchen table."

"What about her inhaler?"

"She didn't take that, either."

"I still don't know why you let her stay at the country house. You should have put her up in a hotel with a damn guard on her door."

"She wanted to go home. I checked the airports. Left men there. She's still in the city. Wait a minute. White Mustang, license MAH-4567."

"That's it. Where are you?"

Hesitation.

"Dammit, Sly, where are you?"

"Oak Hill Cemetery."

"The cemetery?"

"Car's empty."

Merrick glanced at his son. "Sly found her car."

"But where's Mom?"

"Sly, we'll be there in twenty minutes. I just passed the Pentagon." When Merrick hung up, he said, "She's at the cemetary, Erik."

"What's she doing there?"

They had discussed a lot of things over the past two days, but the grave site hadn't been one of them. "I told you Cyrus faked your mother's death."

"I remember." Erik suddenly got the picture. "You think she went to her grave?"

"That's what I think."

"Why?"

"I don't know."

"Are you going to tell her about…Cyrus?"

"Yes."

"Even the part about him wanting me dead?"

Merrick was proud of his son. He'd been through a lot, and he was trying hard to understand a situation that was as difficult to believe as it was to make sense of.

He said, "Cyrus was a good man, once. I'm responsible for leaving him in Prague."

"But not for how he lived after that," Erik said. "He stole Mom from you. Made her think you wanted her dead. Mom taught me that we're responsible for who we are and what we do. You didn't make him do all those bad things. He made that choice."

"Smart woman, your mother."

Erik grinned. "Pretty, too."

"I won't argue with that."

"So you're okay with it?"

"With what, Erik?"

"Having me for your son?"

Merrick glanced at Erik. "I'm okay with it."

Erik looked out the window.

Another glance and Merrick saw his son swallow hard. He said, "How about you? Are you okay with having me in your life?"

Erik glanced at his father, a slow smile settling on his handsome face. "I'm okay with it."

They crossed the Potomac, and ten minutes later Merrick pulled the gray rental behind Johanna's Mustang.

"That's her car?" Erik asked as he got out of the rental.

"You know cars?"

"Not much. More about boats," he admitted. "Never thought she'd drive a hot car."

"Some day I'll tell you about your hot mother," Merrick said, grinning. He saw Sly standing next to the iron gate. His stance was relaxed. He said to Erik, "Mind waiting here? I'd like to—"

"Go on. I think you should see her first."

Merrick nodded, then limped toward the gate, his knee still giving him hell.

"She's at the grave site," Sly said.

"You talk to her?"

"You said you'd be here soon. Thought I'd just sit tight. You look better than I expected. Sully said you were in rough shape." He pulled Johanna's ring from his pocket. "I know you told me to give this to her, but I thought you'd want to put it back on her finger yourself."

Merrick took Johanna's wedding ring. "You knew I'd be back?"

Sly grinned. "Icis die in Greece? Not a chance in hell."

Merrick glanced toward the path. "I think I'll take a couple more days off." He looked back at Sly. "Mind filling in for me a few days longer?"

"Whatever you need, you know I'll be there."

"I know." Merrick reached out and squeezed Sly's arm, then he started down the path. He spotted Johanna on the bench and saw a woman sitting beside her. It was Sarah Finny. Sarah stood, then walked away and headed for the path.

It was Saturday. He'd forgotten that. Merrick glanced at his watch. Sarah should be at work. He watched her come toward him, her blond hair moving around her shoulders.

On a collision course, she saw him halfway to the gate and stopped. Then she came forward, smiling. "She told me she wasn't sure if you were dead or alive."

"I just got back. Guess I'm alive."

"I'm glad you're all right. She's beautiful, Adolf."

"I know. Inside and out."

She reached out and touched his arm. "I'm happy for you. Happy for her, too. I guess this means no more Medallions."

"I think it means I'll be picking them up and bringing them home," he said.

She stepped forward and kissed his cheek, then whispered, "You were right about us. She always had your heart." Then she walked past him.

Merrick didn't look back. His future was sitting on that bench, and his eyes went there to Johanna and the two dozen roses crowning her headstone.

He supposed he would have to explain that, and let her know why Sarah was here. Or maybe Sarah had already done that.

Dressed all in black, he followed the path. The breeze caught his silver hair, and he made a quick swipe through it. He was a little beat-up, but she was used to that.

She never moved from the bench as he turned down the next path. He came up on her from behind, rounded the bench and sat down. It surprised her. Then it shocked her. Then it sent her into tears and into his arms.

They never spoke for several minutes. Just held each other. Finally, he said, "Erik's fine. He's waiting by the car."

She looked up at him with happy tears in her eyes. "I was so afraid, but then I told myself…trust him. Have faith."

He pulled her close, listened to her breathing. It was steady. No shortness of breath. He brushed a kiss over her lips. "I love you, Johanna. Always trust that."

"I know. I'm just beginning to realize how much."

He glanced at the roses. "You mean the Medallions?"

"The roses, and so much more. I'm living in our house."

Merrick winced. "I'm not much of a housekeeper. I don't think I've dusted in…twenty years."

She laughed. "No you haven't, but it's perfect. I think I'll change the curtains."

"I'll help."

"Why didn't you call?"

"I did. Where have you been all night?"

"Driving, then I fell asleep in the car."

"New rule. Don't go anywhere without your cell phone and your inhaler."

"I have one for you, too. Never leave me again. I need to tell you something," she said, a bit tentative. "I don't want any secrets between us, so I—"

"Whatever it is, I promise I won't make an ass out of myself this time."

"After Erik was born I got pregnant again. I…lost the baby. It was a boy."

Merrick pulled her close and kissed her temple. "I'm sorry," he whispered.

She looked up and touched his cheek. Kissed him, then said, "There's something else. I…I've loved you from the day we met, and I've never stopped."

"I know." He smiled down at her, then he lowered his head, and when he kissed her again time stood still.

He wasn't surprised by the question that followed. "How is Erik?"

"Tough kid, our son. Smart, too."

"You said he's at the car?"

"He agreed to give me a few minutes alone with you. He's drooling over his mother's hot car. Guess we're going to have to get him one."

She laughed through her tears. Sobered. "What happened on the island? Is he...dead?"

"What do you want?"

"I want him to never touch us ever again."

It was an ironic choice of words. "Done."

"Then he's dead?"

"No. We ended up going off a cliff. I got lucky. Cyrus ended up paralyzed. He severed his spinal cord. He asked me to kill him. It would have been easy after everything, but until we can locate all his hideouts and contacts, Onyxx needs him alive. I turned him over to EURO-Quest in Prague. I thought it would be better. My supervisors agreed, and so did Lev Polax, Quest's administrator. We've shared a few missions. Cyrus is in good hands."

"Meaning?"

"I'm no saint, Johanna. He's alive, wishing he was dead. That's the hell he's going to have to live with." He wrapped his arm around her and said, "You ready to get out of here?"

"I'm ready to go anywhere with you."

Merrick pulled the ring from his pocket. "Then I guess it's settled." He took her hand and slipped the ring onto her finger. "Let's go home, Mrs. Merrick."

They stood, and hand in hand they walked toward the gate, passed through it.

Erik came toward them, smiling, said, "Cool car, Mom."

Merrick stopped as Johanna moved away from him, rushed to their son and hugged him. He heard her whisper, "I love you so much."

"I love you, too. I want to apologize for what I said to you on the island, Mom."

"You were upset. You had a right to be. Apology accepted. You're sure you're all right?"

Erik's answer was no surprise. Merrick had asked him that question more than once over the past two days. But what he hadn't heard was the one word Erik used now as he stepped back and looked at him.

"I'm okay, Mom. *Dad's* been taking good care of me, and I've been taking good care of him, too."

Johanna turned back, the word sending her into more happy tears.

Merrick said, "Give Erik the keys and climb in the back, Johanna. Erik, you drive and keep your eyes on the road. I'm going to make out in the back seat with your mother."

Johanna angled her head and arched a beautiful eyebrow as if she was going to protest, then she pulled the keys from her pocket and tossed them to their son. "Erik, you drive. I'm going to make out with your father in the back seat." She headed for the car, then turned to look at him. "Second thoughts, dream man?"

He smiled. "Not one."

She smiled back, then climbed in the backseat as Erik slid behind the wheel. Merrick paused a moment and glanced over the hood of the car to the path he'd walked a thousand times over the years. His eyes locked on the Medallions far in the distance, then he ducked his head, climbed into the car and wrapped his arms around his wife.

Later that night, with the crackle and pop of wood burning slow and luminous in the brick fireplace, he waited for her to come to him.

The bed moved against her fragile weight. She curled up beside him and sent her hand slowly over his bare chest, then touched the bandage on his shoulder.

"How do you feel?"

"Like I'm in a dream."

"Me, too."

Her hand slowly moved over his bruised ribs. Lower.

Merrick groaned in appreciation. In anticipation.

She slipped her naked thigh over his hips and straddled him, leaned forward and kissed him. "However you want me, I'm here," she whispered.

"I want you all night. Every night," he said, the dream so clear. So very real. Fully awake, staring into those beautiful eyes, Merrick claimed his wife for all time, whispering, "My love. My wife. My life."

Another kiss.

Another moan.

Forever wrapped in Johanna's arms.

A thousand kisses deep, Merrick and Johanna fell asleep all tangled up, listening to the rain and their hearts beating as one.

Epilogue

Onyxx moved quickly once they had Cyrus Krizova's coerced confession and locked on their targets. As much as he hated leaving Johanna and Erik, Merrick flew to Greece with Sly McEwen and joined his men.

The reconnaissance mission was fast and furious, the largest of its kind in the history of the intelligence world. Within a week they had unearthed Cyrus's two dozen hideouts, a dozen monasteries and billions of dollars in contraband. The sweep was also responsible for the rescue of over a hundred operatives from all over the country who had gone missing and been presumed dead.

As Cyrus's empire fell, so did his powerful associates and several fascist groups bent on global terrorism.

Days later, back in Washington, Merrick left Harry Pendleton's office with an offer on the table. Onyxx wanted him to head up a new division of the Agency that would specialize in recruiting and training a new breed of agents, with Merrick's elite six as the prototype.

It was late afternoon when Merrick drove his Jag out of the parking lot at headquarters and headed for Chadwick's in Georgetown. Sly had called him earlier in the day and asked if they could meet for a drink. Twenty minutes later he walked into the bar wearing black slacks, a gray V-neck sweater and his black leather jacket.

One quick drink, he thought, anxious to get home to Johanna and his son. Johanna would be cooking something fabulous for dinner, and Erik would be cooling his heels waiting for his *dad* to get home. His son liked hanging out with his old man.

Erik was talking about college in the fall. He could draw and paint as beautifully as his mother, but he also had a mean arm when it came to throwing a football in the backyard, and could run a four-minute mile. Whatever he decided to do with his life, he would be great at it. His current passions were fast cars and pretty girls, and he'd been busy shopping for both.

As usual, Chadwick's was crowded. Merrick was a few minutes late, but as he glanced around there was no sign of Sly. He was about to grab a booth when he spotted Johanna in an alcove that led down a back hall. She was leaning against the wall, smiling at him.

That smile brought back a poignant memory of the first time he'd seen her. It had been here at Chadwick's over twenty-five years ago, and her beautiful smile had touched his soul that day. It touched him now.

She was dressed for dinner in a gold strapless dress that hugged her amazing curves. A gold-threaded shawl was draped low over her shoulders, and she had a pair of gold high-heel sandals on her pretty feet. She'd done something different with her long black hair. She'd pulled half of it up, leaving naughty, sexy bangs to tease her hazel-green eyes.

He walked toward her, wishing they were home. As much

as he liked what she was wearing, his fingers were itching to strip her naked and take her to bed.

"I know what you're thinking," she said when he stopped and shouldered into the wall, one hand in his pocket.

"You think so?"

She leaned close and kissed him, then whispered, "The dream man has me naked. Are we in bed, or on the rug in front of the fireplace?"

"You pick."

She kissed him again, teased his lower lip. "So why did you want to meet me here instead of at home?"

"Meet here?" Merrick arched an eyebrow. "Who told you that?"

"Sly called and said you wanted me to dress for dinner and meet you at Chadwick's."

Merrick pulled his hand from his pocket and slid it around her and brought her against him. She smelled good, and he was tempted to drag her into the bathroom and lock the door. Instead, he whispered, "I think there's a conspiracy going on."

"A conspiracy?"

"I smell a rat. Sly say anything else?"

Her hand moved slowly over his chest, her fingers finding the open V of his sweater. "Only that you'd arranged a private dinner for two." She pointed over her shoulder down the hall to a closed door.

Merrick glanced at the door, then shoved away from the wall and turned her slowly, keeping his arm around her. "I think we've been conned, Johanna, but I'm willing to play. Come on. Let's see what Sly's up to."

They walked to the end of the hall, and without hesitation Merrick swung open the door. The room was dark, the light from the hall casting a dim glow over a long table surrounded by chairs. Suddenly the lights came on and a round of applause echoed throughout the room.

Merrick stared into the faces of his men lined up along the

far wall. Sly McEwen, Bjorn Odell, Jacy Madox, Pierce Fourtier, Ash Kelly and Sully Paxton. They were all there. All wearing grins standing beside their women—Eva Creon, Nadja Stefn, Prisca Reznik, Casmir Balasi, Jazmin Grant and Melita Krizova.

It was a moment he would never forget. A reunion that would be remembered and cherished for years to come. And in that moment Merrick felt a pride that shook him to the core, and he knew without a doubt what his answer would be when Harry Pendleton called him in a few days. The Onyxx's Rat Fighters would live on.

He felt a hand on his shoulder as someone came up behind him. It was Erik, and he wrapped his arm around his son and ushered him and Johanna forward. "Come on," he said, "I want you two to meet your extended family. They're one helluva group. The best I've ever known."

Hours later, seated around the table, Sly raised his glass and everyone responded in kind. "To Merrick and Johanna," he said. "To a long future of happiness. No one deserves it more."

Merrick stood and followed the toast with one of his own. He raised his glass and said, "To good friends and loyal comrades and—" he glanced around the table at each one of his men and the beautiful women seated beside them, then down at Johanna "—to the brave women who love us. Love deep, with all their hearts. Know we love just as deeply. To the end, and beyond."

Six months later in Prague

Deep in the bowels of the Vysehrad Museum, Merrick walked down the corridor at EURO-Quest with Lev Polax at his side.

Lev said, "He's asked for you every day. What has Onyxx decided to do with Cyrus Krizova?"

"Onyxx has left it up to me," Merrick said.

He had been putting off the trip. He'd spent the past months focused on being the best husband and father he could be, and building the new division of Onyxx that would soon be known as SARF—Special Agent Rat Fighters. Every one of his men, the original six, had come on board in one capacity or another. The project was off the ground and they had recruited ten candidates.

They stopped outside the door where Cyrus had been existing on hand-fed meals with cameras watching his every move. Polax pulled a key from his pocket and handed it to Merrick. "And what's your decision? Do you plan to grant him his wish?"

"I'll see you before I leave."

"Whatever you decide, you know I'll support it. I'll be in my office."

As EURO-Quest's commander walked away, Merrick inserted the key in the lock and opened the door. He was expecting to see Cyrus on his back, the way he'd left him months ago, but he was seated in a wheelchair, his body strapped in, his head crowned in stainless steel to support his neck.

At first he thought Cyrus was asleep, but he opened his eyes as Merrick entered.

"It's about time you got here."

"I've been busy," Merrick said. "Busy tearing down your empire."

"Onyxx must be slipping if it took this long. Or perhaps you've been too busy enjoying the rewards of your victory. By the way, how is Callia?"

Merrick had planned to keep Johanna out of the conversation, but as he looked at his enemy trapped in iron, he realized that Cyrus was a broken man existing on memories.

Memories… He'd survived on memories for years. They were what had kept him alive.

He said, "Johanna is well and as beautiful as ever."

"*Da,* beautiful. The first time I saw her I envied you. Even before you left me in that minefield, I wanted what you had. The day I took Johanna I was going to kill her, but she was too beautiful to kill, so I made her mine and gave her a new name."

"A new name doesn't change fact. Johanna was never yours."

"Are you going to desert me again like you did in Prague? Leave me here alive praying for death? Or have you come to do what you should have done years ago?"

"I was wrong that day. But my mistake does not exonerate your terror and destruction, Cyrus. So much suffering. So much senseless pain and death."

"I suffered pain."

"And survived it. Why wasn't that enough?"

"I'm beyond shame, Merrick. If that is your goal, you waste your time and mine. Finish me. Get it over with and then leave me in peace."

"You want peace now?" Merrick shook his head. "To give you what you ask for would mean I forgive you for the lives you destroyed. I can't forget, and I refuse to forgive."

"You didn't come all this way to refuse me. You won't walk out on me again. I gave you what you asked for months ago. We had a deal. Set me free, Merrick. You owe me."

"If you want to die, make a deal with God. Only he has the power to set you free. Not me."

Merrick turned to leave.

"Come back and finish me, you bastard. Come back, Merrick! This is no life, rotting in this chair. I can't live like this."

Merrick stopped. "Then pray harder, and make your peace with the only one who can forgive you and take you from this world. I won't play God. I won't kill you." He started to leave again, then stopped once more. "Oh, I saw Sully and Melita a few days ago. You have a grandson. They named him... Patrick Adolf Paxton."

Merrick walked out the door and, as he closed it and

inserted the key into the lock, he could hear Cyrus screaming his name. He could still hear him as he walked down the hall and through a set of steel doors.

He stopped by Lev Polax's office to let him know how things stood. They shook hands, and then he was on a flight back to Washington. Back to Johanna and Erik.

He closed his gray eyes, warming to the image of his wife, anxious to be home. He slept as the plane crossed the ocean. Slept holding Johanna close in the dream, her arms wrapped around him and her sweet lips whispering his name.

He reached the country house early in the morning. He parked in the driveway and, as he stood in the morning sunlight, his eyes drifted to the corner of the house. Johanna stood in the rose garden, her hand holding back her long black hair as she inhaled the sweet scent of a perfect yellow rose.

Like the sea's love affair with the shore, theirs was a love unending. An affair of the heart no man could destroy.

One love. One soul mate. One life together…forever.

* * * * *

Silhouette Desire kicks off 2009 with
MAN OF THE MONTH, *a yearlong program featuring incredible heroes by stellar authors.*

When navy SEAL Hunter Cabot returns home for some much-needed R & R, he discovers he's a married man. There's just one problem: he's never met his "bride."

Enjoy this sneak peek at Maureen Child's
AN OFFICER AND A MILLIONAIRE.
Available January 2009 from Silhouette Desire.

One

Hunter Cabot, Navy SEAL, had a healing bullet wound in his side, thirty days' leave and, apparently, a wife he'd never met.

On the drive into his hometown of Springville, California, he stopped for gas at Charlie Evans's service station. That's where the trouble started.

"Hunter! Man, it's good to see you! Margie didn't tell us you were coming home."

"Margie?" Hunter leaned back against the front fender of his black pickup truck and winced as his side gave a small twinge of pain. Silently then, he watched as the man he'd known since high school filled his tank.

Charlie grinned, shook his head and pumped gas. "Guess your wife was lookin' for a little 'alone' time with you, huh?"

"My—" Hunter couldn't even say the word. *Wife?* He didn't have a wife. "Look, Charlie..."

"Don't blame her, of course," his friend said with a wink

as he finished up and put the gas cap back on. "You being gone all the time with the SEALs must be hard on the ol' love life."

He'd never had any complaints, Hunter thought, frowning at the man still talking a mile a minute. "What're you—"

"Bet Margie's anxious to see you. She told us all about that R and R trip you two took to Bali." Charlie's dark brown eyebrows lifted and wiggled.

"Charlie..."

"Hey, it's okay, you don't have to say a thing, man."

What the hell could he say? Hunter shook his head, paid for his gas and as he left, told himself Charlie was just losing it. Maybe the guy had been smelling gas fumes too long.

But as it turned out, it wasn't just Charlie. Stopped at a red light on Main Street, Hunter glanced out his window to smile at Mrs. Harker, his second-grade teacher who was now at least a hundred years old. In the middle of the crosswalk, the old lady stopped and shouted, "Hunter Cabot, you've got yourself a wonderful wife. I hope you appreciate her."

Scowling now, he only nodded at the old woman—the only teacher who'd ever scared the crap out of him. What the hell was going on here? Was everyone but him nuts?

His temper beginning to boil, he put up with a few more comments about his "wife" on the drive through town before finally pulling into the wide, circular drive leading to the Cabot mansion. Hunter didn't have a clue what was going on, but he planned to get to the bottom of it. Fast.

He grabbed his duffel bag, stalked into the house and paid no attention to the housekeeper, who ran at him, fluttering both hands. "Mr. Hunter!"

"Sorry, Sophie," he called out over his shoulder as he took the stairs two at a time. "Need a shower, then we'll talk."

He marched down the long, carpeted hallway to the rooms that were always kept ready for him. In his suite, Hunter tossed the duffel down and stopped dead. The shower in his bathroom was running. His *wife?*

Anger and curiosity boiled in his gut, creating a churning mass that had him moving forward without even thinking about it. He opened the bathroom door to a wall of steam and the sound of a woman singing—off-key. Margie, no doubt.

Well, if she was his wife...Hunter walked across the room, yanked the shower door open and stared in at a curvy, naked, temptingly wet woman.

She whirled to face him, slapping her arms across her naked body while she gave a short, terrified scream.

Hunter smiled. "Hi, honey. I'm home."

* * * * *

Be sure to look for
AN OFFICER AND A MILLIONAIRE
by USA TODAY bestselling author Maureen Child.
Available January 2009 from Silhouette Desire.

CELEBRATE 60 YEARS
OF PURE READING PLEASURE
WITH HARLEQUIN®!

We'll be spotlighting a different series
every month throughout 2009
to celebrate our 60th anniversary.
Look for Silhouette Desire® in January!

Collect all 12 books in the Silhouette Desire®
Man of the Month continuity, starting in
January 2009 with *An Officer and a Millionaire*
by *USA TODAY* bestselling author
Maureen Child.

*Look for one new Man of the Month title
every month in 2009!*

REQUEST YOUR FREE BOOKS!

2 FREE NOVELS PLUS 2 FREE GIFTS!

Silhouette® Romantic

SUSPENSE

Sparked by Danger, Fueled by Passion!

YES! Please send me 2 FREE Silhouette® Romantic Suspense novels and my 2 FREE gifts (gifts are worth about $10). After receiving them, if I don't wish to receive any more books, I can return the shipping statement marked "cancel." If I don't cancel, I will receive 4 brand-new novels every month and be billed just $4.24 per book in the U.S. or $4.99 per book in Canada, plus 25¢ shipping and handling per book plus applicable taxes, if any*. That's a savings of at least 15% off the cover price! I understand that accepting the 2 free books and gifts places me under no obligation to buy anything. I can always return a shipment and cancel at any time. Even if I never buy another book from Silhouette, the two free books and gifts are mine to keep forever.

240 SDN EEX6   340 SDN EEYJ

Name	(PLEASE PRINT)	
Address		Apt. #
City	State/Prov.	Zip/Postal Code

Signature (if under 18, a parent or guardian must sign)

Mail to the Silhouette Reader Service:
IN U.S.A.: P.O. Box 1867, Buffalo, NY 14240-1867
IN CANADA: P.O. Box 609, Fort Erie, Ontario L2A 5X3

Not valid to current subscribers of Silhouette Romantic Suspense books.

Want to try two free books from another line?
Call 1-800-873-8635 or visit www.morefreebooks.com.

* Terms and prices subject to change without notice. N.Y. residents add applicable sales tax. Canadian residents will be charged applicable provincial taxes and GST. Offer not valid in Quebec. This offer is limited to one order per household. All orders subject to approval. Credit or debit balances in a customer's account(s) may be offset by any other outstanding balance owed by or to the customer. Please allow 4 to 6 weeks for delivery. Offer available while quantities last.

Your Privacy: Silhouette is committed to protecting your privacy. Our Privacy Policy is available online at www.eHarlequin.com or upon request from the Reader Service. From time to time we make our lists of customers available to reputable third parties who may have a product or service of interest to you. If you would prefer we not share your name and address, please check here. ☐

SRS08R

Silhouette®
Romantic
SUSPENSE

COMING NEXT MONTH

#1543 BOUNTY HUNTER'S WOMAN—Linda Turner
Broken Arrow Ranch

Hired as her bodyguard, bounty hunter Donovan Jones hasn't even met Priscilla Wyatt before she's kidnapped and he has to rescue her. Priscilla is wary of Donovan's true intentions, but she'll have to learn to put her life—and her heart—in his hands if she wants to save her family's ranch in time.

#1544 BABY'S WATCH—Justine Davis
The Coltons: Family First

Former bad boy Ryder Colton has never felt a connection to much, so he's shocked when he feels one to the baby he helps deliver, as well as her mother. Ana Morales doesn't quite trust this stranger, but when her daughter is taken by a smuggling ring, she teams up with him to rescue the baby. Will they put their lives on the line for love?

#1545 TERMS OF ENGAGEMENT—Kylie Brant
Alpha Squad

On the run from a hit man, Lindsay Bradford's bravery in a hostage situation puts her picture on the news, and now she must flee again. But after they share a passionate night, Detective Jack Langley won't let her go. She never thought she'd trust another cop to help her, but Lindsay finally risks everything when she puts her trust in Jack….

#1546 BURNING SECRETS—Elizabeth Sinclair

When forest ranger Jesse Kingston is sent on forced leave after his best friend dies in a firestorm, he returns home to find himself face-to-face with Karen Ellis—the woman who's carrying his friend's baby. Both suspicious about the man's death, they join together to discover the truth—about the fire and about their hearts' deepest desires.